SERRA ROSE

Heart of the Wolf

First published in 2025 by Serra Rose in Melbourne, Australia.

Editing: Ellen Klowden

Proofreader: Jess M.B

Cover design by Miblart

For permissions, inquiries, or further information, please contact through:

www.serrarosewrites.com

First edition

ISBN: 978-1-7638448-5-8

This book was professionally typeset on Reedsy.
Find out more at reedsy.com

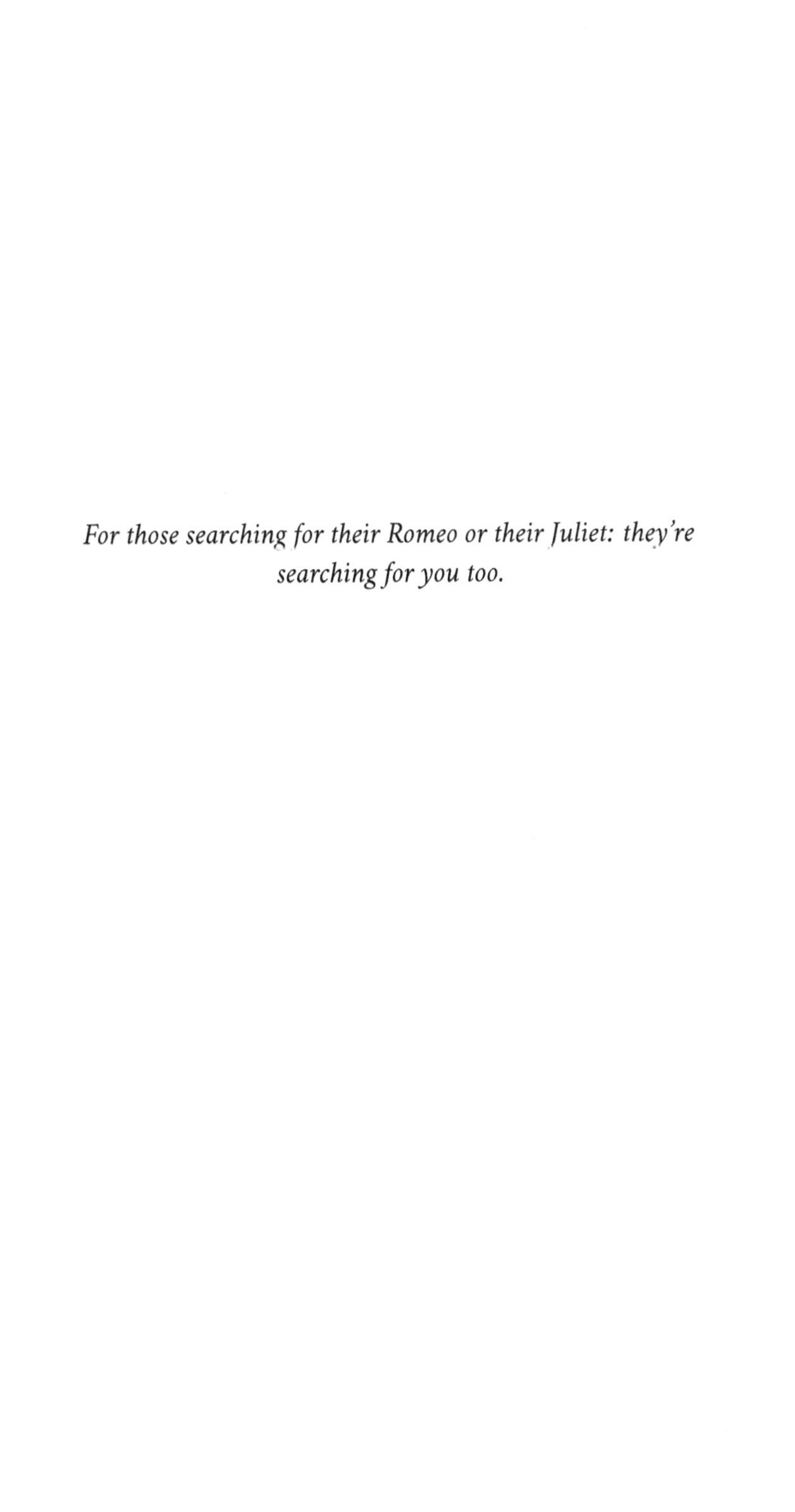

For those searching for their Romeo or their Juliet: they're searching for you too.

These violent delights have violent
ends
And in their triumph die like fire and
powder,
Which, as they kiss, consume.

Romeo and Juliet - William
Shakespeare

Contents

Content Warning

This book is intended for readers who are 18+. It contains detailed scenes of consensual sexual intimacy. It also includes themes and scenes that may be triggering for some readers.

Death of a deer in a hunting scene between two wolves
    Description of wolves tearing into deer to eat
    Brutal, animalistic deaths of characters
    Marking without consent (Not between MCs)
    Defensive territorial behaviour
    Death and dealing with grief
    Loss
    Funeral
    Claustrophobic setting in a cave
    Consensual Chasing
    Nudity
    Crushing/bone breaking
    Stalking

Be kind to yourself. Your mental health matters.

Glossary

Swanndri or swanny - a popular outdoor clothing brand in New Zealand; in the case of this story, a woollen jacket. Popular in rural areas.

Triple one - NZ emergency number.

Hi-lux - Toyota Hi-lux: a type of vehicle.

Ute - utility truck.

Bush - dense native forests in New Zealand.

Author's note

Heart of the Wolf is set in New Zealand. I have not named where in New Zealand, as that isn't really part of my characters' world. Their world is about their pack, their territory, and just being wolves. The human world is something they rarely delve into.

This book is written in British English. We use U a lot in words, like rumour, and sometimes S instead of Z, such as in recognise.

Chapter 1

ROMAN

I longed to be running with my pack, to howl. The moon would be full the following night; her energy was already buzzing through my blood. My wolf had risen close to the surface, the need for us to be one, enjoying the thrill of the hunt, surrounded by others. That irresistible pull to shift would only grow stronger as the full moon neared. There was nothing quite like that freedom, to be unburdened by the expectations of the human world.

Instead, I was in human form. Clothes brushed against my skin, denim and wool; heavy, rough, and unnatural. Yet without my fur, I felt naked. As we climbed out of my black twin cab Toyota hi-lux, Mason, my beta, pulled his beanie over his silver hair, placing sunglasses over his yellow eyes. I grabbed my beanie, covering my own eyes with sunnies. Many wolves used contacts to disguise their eyes, but I found them uncomfortable, and I could never decide on an eye colour I liked.

Mason breathed into his cupped hands to warm them. "Fuck, it's freezing," he complained.

I grabbed hand warmers from the seat and threw them at him, grinning.

He laughed. "I can always count on you to have something useful."

I locked the ute and zipped up my Swanndri, then we started walking across the car park.

"Maybe you should buy some gloves while we're here!" I joked.

He scoffed.

I hated being in human form. Even with supernatural reflexes, strength, and speed, it lacked the freedom of being a wolf. I couldn't be myself around the humans, and it was easy to forget to move the way they did. "Remember, loud steps," I said. "Be like a human."

"They're such ungraceful creatures." Mason sighed. "My wolf yearns to run," he said as we walked. "Especially this close to the full moon. I know we don't have to come into the town very often, but it just makes me uneasy. I feel trapped."

I couldn't blame him. I felt the same. Centuries before, our ancestors had avoided human villages and cities. We didn't belong living among them. But times had changed, and it had become a necessity to exist alongside their world.

"We won't be long," I promised. "We can go home soon."

"Oh! Maybe Rosie's working today!" Mason said, turning and playfully hitting me on the chest. "Roooossssieeee?!"

"Stop!" I laughed, pushing him away.

He punched me in the shoulder. "What? You're not afraid she'll hear me, are you?" He shook his head. "Human hearing is so limited!"

I swatted his hands away as he jabbed at me again.

We reached the door, which Mason pulled open. "After you, lover boy!" he joked.

I shook my head, chuckling, and entered the hardware shop. Mason had said it himself: we didn't come here often, but sometimes it was just necessary. My family provided for much of the town, and we were well known amongst the humans. It excited them to catch a glimpse of us. Three other humans were in the shop.

A series of scents hit me all at once. The vanilla perfume of Rosie. Earth, lumber, metal, sweat, and cooked meat. I suppressed the urge to gag. Humans didn't have the stomach for raw meat, and I didn't understand how they enjoyed such dry food. They also didn't have the teeth to tear into it the way wolves did. Once again, I felt sorry that humans were unable to enjoy life's delicacies, forced to cook their food and cut it up.

"Roman!" A woman's voice called out as I walked into the

shop. "My favourite farm boy! Long time, no see! You've grown out a bit of a beard! Nice."

I gave Rosie my widest smile. She had strawberry-blonde hair and brown eyes; a slight woman with bubbly energy. "Rosie, as beautiful as ever!" I remarked. "Did you get a haircut?"

She beamed at me, her eyes sparkling, her cheeks turning a shade of pink. "I did. I thought men didn't notice stuff like that." She looked me up and down. "I feel like you get hotter every time I see you," she remarked. "You're like a fine wine."

Our harmless flirting caught the attention of the cashier. "She's not wrong," he said. "The sunglasses add mystery. That scruff and long hair definitely have rugged farm boy vibes!"

I laughed. Mason chuckled beside me, elbowing me in the ribs, eyeing the cashier.

"I haven't seen you here before. Are you new?" Mason asked him.

"I am." The cashier smiled at Mason. "Are you his friend?"

"I'm his be-uhh, I work with him. *For* him." Mason stopped himself from declaring to humans that he was my beta, adhering to the story we used for them.

I almost rolled my eyes. Mason rarely fumbled over his words. He turned to me with a grin and mouthed, 'Cute.'

"So what brings the most eligible bachelor into town today?" Rosie asked.

If I'd been human, I probably would have considered Rosie, given her a home and maybe even children. She had a kind heart, and a gentleness about her. But as a wolf, any cubs would either be fully human, the thought of which only saddened me, or permanently stuck between human and wolf. A beastly creature that would cause issues for my people. Deterring wolf-human mating was the wolf goddess's attempt to keep our lineage strong. We avoided pairing with humans, and very rarely did the Goddess choose a human mate for wolves. It was risky, bringing them into our world. They didn't always survive our bite. I would never do that to a human.

Like my parents, I would co-alpha the pack, and my firstborn would one day rise to be the next alpha after me. But it didn't stop me hitting on Rosie. I enjoyed our banter, and I never had a feeling of more than amusement from her. If I'd thought for a moment she expected more, I would have let her down gently. It wasn't my nature to give anyone false hope.

"I need some iron gates," I said. "Trellis. And wire. The storm last week caused damage."

Rosie led us away. Mason glanced over his shoulder towards the cashier, his signature flirtatious smile on display. This time I elbowed Mason, and he simply winked at me. Rosie helped us find what we needed, and I added barbed wire to my order.

I approached the counter just as Tyler Carpenter entered the shop. The second he walked in, I caught his scent. Mason and I turned our heads towards the door in unison. Like us, Tyler wore sunglasses to cover his yellow wolf eyes. He had a maroon beanie with 'Silver Moon Farms', the name of his pack, across the front. Light brown hair showed from the edges. His Swanndri was red and black, a contrast to my and Mason's green and black chequered swannies. Our black beanies had the words 'Midnight Farms'; my pack name, across the front, with the crescent moon as our logo.

"Time for us to leave," Mason said as he handed over the card. "Before that dick decides to cause trouble."

Tyler turned towards us and smirked.

"Good morning, cubs," he said. Even from the other side

of the shop, the words were clear. Mason was right. Time to leave.

Unfortunately, leaving was more complicated than it should have been. We'd just purchased four wrought-iron gates, which to a human would be too heavy to carry out without assistance. So we were forced to push the trolley we'd placed the gates on. If Tyler was here, it was likely others of his pack were too. Especially his betas.

Tyler stood in our way, preventing us from passing through. I stepped away from the trolley, advancing on him. We stood inches apart.

"Move," I ordered in a low voice, adding my wolf's growl to the tone.

Tyler crossed his arms over his chest, smirking again.

We both would have bared our teeth at each other, and had we broken into a fight, it would not have been one appropriate with human witnesses. I picked up the sound of Rosie walking around the aisles with a human, and the cashier had headphones on, his music blasting through. I showed Tyler my canines, letting them lengthen enough without shifting.

Mason stepped up beside me. "He said, 'move'!"

Tyler tilted his head towards Mason. "You think to give an alpha commands, beta?" he asked quietly.

"You're not alpha *yet*," I reminded him. "You need a mate for that."

"Where's *your* mate then, little pup?" Tyler said.

"Are you going to move? Or do I have to move you myself?" I challenged.

Tyler was older and larger than me, and to threaten him would prove foolish if I wasn't careful.

The approaching full moon, mixed with anger at Tyler's

blatant challenge in the presence of humans, brought my wolf even closer to the surface, and a growl broke free. Mason grabbed my arm and pulled me back.

"Tyler, why are you such a fucking dick?" Mason asked. "Just get out of the way, so we can go home. Unlike you, who clearly has too much time on his hands, we actually have work to do."

Behind the trolley, Mason pushed forward. Tyler must have thought better than going up against a charging Mason, and he finally stepped aside.

Tyler's chuckle came through the door right before it closed behind us. Relieved to find the car park almost empty, I paused, taking in deep breaths. I knew better than to let myself be pulled into such emotions. Mason stood beside me in silence, waiting for me to compose myself.

Finally, we returned to my ute. Splattered with mud, it was definitely not a vehicle that fit in with the cars that surrounded it. Tyler's black sports car with flames across the front blocked me in. I rolled my eyes. *Jackass.* This time, I kept my anger at bay.

"Arrogant shit," Mason said. "Him and that hideous car."

I laughed. "What I wouldn't give to piss on the tyre. Wipe that smirk off his damn face."

"Do it!" Mason challenged.

"Tempting." I glanced back at the car, then at the shop, "Not while I'm in public. I don't need the cops charging me for indecent exposure or some shit," I said.

"Hey! I was a cub!" he declared, laughing. "It was my first shift. How was I supposed to know the humans were afraid of nudity!"

I shook my head in amusement. He was right, though. Discovering that humans wore clothes had been an adjustment.

So as to not reveal our strength, it was a slow task of unloading the iron gates, both of us lifting each gate between us. Once the back was loaded, I jumped in the cab.

"Roman." Mason's voice from outside grabbed my attention before I could start the engine. Almost as if he were speaking through gritted teeth.

His focus was on the side of the ute.

Curious, I climbed out and walked around. A growl broke free when I saw deep claw marks across the passenger door over the Midnight Farms logo.

"Oh, for fuck's sake," I growled. "It's always something with him!"

Mason glanced around the car park and lifted his sunglasses. His yellow eyes were filled with mischief. "If that's the game he wants to play...keep an eye out!"

He confidently walked towards Tyler's car as I examined the claw marks in the ute. They were deep, angry. It wouldn't be easy to fix.

I winced at the sound of metal screeching. As Mason grinned up at me, sheer joy shone from his eyes. Watching the door of the shop, I noticed he was doing a lot more damage than I'd anticipated.

"Are you writing something?" I asked.

Mason laughed. "I'm writing 'dick'."

"Hurry up!" I warned him. "If he catches us, there'll be hell to pay."

"Then make him pay for what he did to the ute," Mason replied.

Finally he was done, and he jumped into the passenger seat beside me. I backed over the barrier, both of us laughing. Tyler came out of the shop, grinning as we drove past. I almost wished I could wait to see his expression when he saw his car.

"Oh, he's going to be pissed!" I chuckled. "He'll probably give chase, as if he can take on my ute."

"He's about to be more pissed when he realises I shredded his back tyre too!" Mason grinned, turning around to look out the back window. "Chasing is not possible."

I scoffed. "Yeah, you probably shouldn't have done that."

Mason shrugged. "He had it coming."

Chapter 2

ROMAN

"I hope our little stunt doesn't get back to my parents," I said, my mood becoming sombre. "I'll be alpha soon. I'm supposed to show them I can lead peacefully, without letting my emotions rule."

We passed five houses that had been built near our territory. The human world was ever expanding, and it worried me. In a few generations, it would be impossible to hide our existence from humans. Wolves were not native wildlife to New Zealand, so that would create problems for shifters.

"Please!" Mason wound the window down. "You can lead peacefully. You didn't do anything, *I* did! My brother, you escape responsibility for this one!" He grinned at me. "Besides, as you reminded Tyler, you need a mate before you can officially step into those paws."

We approached large gates with high rock walls that indicated where our territory started. 'Midnight Farms' was fixed in large letters between the columns of the gate. I stopped the ute. Mason leaned his head out the window and let out a howl, letting the pack know we were approaching. Three returning howls echoed back.

"One of these days the humans are going to stop believing our claim that we have a lot of dogs, and realise they're surrounded by wolves," I commented as we paused at the gates.

"Just have Spencer compel them," Mason said with laughter. "We're not causing any harm. We eat what we kill and don't keep trophies, and we look after our land. They only care about money."

He was right. Humans were destructive in ways that worried many wolves. Destroying the land for the sake of money. Wolf shifters had arrived and lived in harmony with the Māori people. We still did, and it was difficult to watch cities expand over beautiful land. We all feared the day humanity discovered us. Hunters already knew of our existence, but their main focus was vampires.

"You know they won't see it that way," I pointed out. "Humans are intolerant of anyone different to them. They will not react well to the knowledge of people stronger and faster than them who can shift into wolves."

Through the dark trees, three wolves moved swiftly towards us. My cousin Bennett led Gideon and Tobias. The rest of my betas, all of them, alongside Mason, had sworn oaths to protect me, and they would be my 'inner circle' when I became alpha. Bennett pushed his head against the gate, which then started to open. Before we could drive through, a wolf moved fast, hitting Tobias hard and taking him down. Another moved forward to attack Gideon as Bennett faced the first wolf

"What the fuck was that?" I demanded, reaching for the door handle.

"Don't," Mason warned. "If that's the Silver Moons, they'll attack you. That's their point."

I growled. "So, what? I watch them attack my betas?"

"Be a lover, not a fighter," Mason said. "You can't get involved, Roman. Our job is to protect you. Keep driving."

Bennett was locked in a fight, Tobias still winded. Gideon snapped at his opponent, who was trying to go for his throat. Deep growls reached us, and I clenched the wheel tight, my knuckles white. Mason let another howl out the window, a more urgent one, letting the pack know there was trouble. Jaws snapped, snarls rose from the fighting wolves. Someone yelped in pain. Bennett leapt at the grey wolf facing him. I recognised the attackers as Tyler's betas.

"If I'm to be alpha, will I really be one to watch his pack get hurt?" I asked Mason as more wolves darted through the trees. Not just Midnight wolves, but Silver Moons, too. "Why are they on our territory?"

I clenched my jaw, my throat closing up.

"Just, don't leave the truck," Mason said. "The alphas will be watching how you react."

Bennett shifted to his human form. "Why do you start a fight on our territory?" he shouted. "Stand down! Put away your claws and fangs. You have no idea what you're doing."

One of the Silver Moons responded by lunging at Bennett. Tobias leapt in the way, blocking the attack. More growls erupted as my pack arrived for backup.

I left my ute, ignoring Mason calling my name. Fumbling with the zip to my Swanndri, I ran straight into a fist. Pain exploded in my face, my cheekbone shattering. Bennett wrapped his arm around the throat of my attacker.

"You hit our alpha," Bennett declared. "I should tear your throat out for that."

My anger rose up, dark and suffocating as I fought to hold my wolf back. Black fur spread across my arms as I ran forward again.

"This isn't your fight," Mason urged, catching up and grabbing my arm. "You get caught in this, it's a bad look for you. The alphas will make an example out of you."

I growled, snapping at him, pulling my arm out of his grip.

Mason cursed under his breath. I followed his gaze to see the reason for his reaction. The humans who lived nearby had heard the commotion. They were on the road to investigate.

"Are those wolves?" someone muttered. I didn't recognise him, so he'd probably just moved in.

"Don't be ridiculous! We don't have wolves in New Zealand," another shot back. "The Morrison family just have a lot of dogs."

Shit. There was no stopping this getting back to the rest of the pack now. Especially to my mother. Co-alpha of the pack, she was very firm about one thing: Don't expose yourself to the humans.

A new wolf arrived, which I immediately recognised as Tyler. Now we were screwed. He was an aggressive wolf, and darted straight for my cousin. But he stopped before making contact and shifted to human form.

"What's going on here then?" Tyler asked his betas. "You haven't taken these inferior creatures yet?" He raised his eyes to me. "Pussy cats. Maybe you're not worthy of our time. The alpha in line takes a strike and does nothing."

Bennett stepped towards Tyler. "I told your beta to stand down. You're on our territory."

Tyler bared his teeth at Bennett. "Stand down? You give orders to that which is not yours to command. I'm their alpha! You want to fight, then face me! I'll tear you apart. Midnight Pack fuckers."

"Stop," I insisted to Tyler. "We're in human presence. You'll expose us all. They're watching."

Tyler glanced back towards where the humans were talking about dogs fighting. It sounded like someone had called triple one. *Great, we'd have the cops out here asking about our dogs.*

My betas formed a circle around me, closing in to protect me.

"What do you want?" I demanded.

Tyler smirked. "Trying to stall? Or are you afraid to fight a real wolf?"

I growled. "I'm not the one picking a fight on another wolf's territory." I pointed at his betas. "They don't come onto our territory without a command. Yours. Is this really what you want?"

Tyler advanced towards me. "Yes."

My betas tightened their formation, growling. Mason stood in front of me.

"Why? We've managed to keep peace; why do you come onto our territory? Out of possible mates, so you're looking for someone desperate enough to let you mark her? You'll find no wolf here with such ideas."

Fury flashed in his eyes.

"You think I want peace?" Tyler grunted. "Or a Midnight bitch?"

"Then you want your throat ripped out," I threatened. "Because I will defend my pack and my territory."

He pointed around us. "I want what's yours. I want you dead, and your pack to submit. Or die with you."

"You won't get what is mine with such a demand." I informed him. His threats to my pack only added to my growing rage.

I growled, my wolf demanding that I let him out. He howled in fury, finally pushing through. Fur rippled across my skin again, my form shifting. The shiver ran down my spine and through my entire body. Bones crunched as they reshaped, muscles stretched. My ears moved from the side of my head to the top, changing shape. My face morphed into that of the wolf, and my tail formed. The shift was over in a few seconds, my body flooded with warmth in the process.

Now one with my wolf, instinct rose up, taking over, becoming primal as I faced Tyler.

"Damn it, Roman," Mason grunted.

Tyler grinned. This was what he'd been aiming for. I'd let myself be goaded into shifting, so he could attack. More wolves arrived, including the alphas. My parents. *Fuck.* But they weren't focused on me; their attention was on the new arrivals through the forest from the west. My Mum was a black wolf like me, but her eyes were silver. My Dad had gained the silver eyes when he'd become her co-alpha, his fur brown. Mum lowered her head, baring her teeth. Her betas surrounded them both.

I caught a new scent; the vampire approaching drew all our attention. Spencer Prince. A man who looked to be in his thirties, but was hundreds of years old. He was taller than me, with a kind face when he wasn't glaring like he was in that moment. He'd been with my pack for a few generations. Sent to watch over us by The Immortal Wolf — an old vampire declared an official pack member centuries ago. Spencer often stepped in when the pack's feud got out of control. He lived nearby, the humans not even aware of his existence.

"All of you, fucking sit down or lie down!" His deep voice boomed out, fangs on display. I had no doubt that behind his magically enhanced, darkened sunglasses; his eyes were red. "You disturb my peace when I'm trying to sleep. Behaving like dogs out in view of the public?" He faced the Silver Moons. "Leave, now. All of you! Or heads will roll." He turned towards us. "You too. Fangs and claws away!"

The Silver Moon wolves backed off. They held respect for Spencer, as he protected all our existence from the humans. I shifted back to human form. My parents only glared at us, before turning and running into the direction of their house. I shuffled towards my ute. Spencer moved towards the humans. It was useful having a vampire around, with an interest in keeping both our worlds hidden.

"I told you," Mason said. "You're supposed to stay out of territory fights. You're better than that, Roman. You let Tyler provoke you."

As I climbed in the cab, adrenaline still flooded my system.

"I only want peace, to co-exist. We're wolves at war with other wolves. We can find peace."

Mason shook his head. "I know you love to find hope in every situation, and I love that about you. But I don't think things will change between our packs. There will be no peace, Tyler doesn't want it."

Wolves were surrounding Tobias, and Gideon whimpered, lifting his eyes towards me. I left the ute and ran over to check on Tobias. His fur was matted, the scent of blood heavy. Mason crouched beside me.

"Help me," I said. "Get him in the back of the ute. Mason, call Solstice."

Gideon shifted, and the four of us carried Tobias, still in wolf form, into the flat deck. He tried to stand, but collapsed onto his side, whimpering. I brushed a hand through his coat, finding his wounds.

"Don't try to move," I said, pushing down the panic. I needed to be calm so he would remain so.

My chest tightened, guilt weighed down on me. Tobias was hurt protecting me. His eyes bored into mine and he panted, dropping his head. Mason, Bennett and Gideon climbed in next to him. The rest of the pack ran towards the farmhouse, howling. I jumped back into the ute as Mason called the Magic Wielder, urgency in his voice.

Chapter 3

JEWEL

The wind caressed my fur as I ran. I stopped at the river to drink, the water cold yet refreshing. Exhilaration burst within me, and I turned my muzzle upward, letting out a long, joyful howl. As other Wilds nearby responded, their baying reverberated through my chest. An animal bolted from the bush, and my desire to give chase flared. My mouth watered at the idea of fresh rabbit as I gave in to the thrill of the hunt. I charged after the small animal. I turned, determined not to let it escape, as it ducked and weaved, evading capture.

I caught a new scent. Another wolf. A small, black and silver wolf stood in my path, allowing the rabbit to escape through her legs. Two young cubs bounded after the rabbit playfully but didn't chase it very far.

I bared my teeth, snapping at the offending wolf. She let her mouth drop into a smile, making a sound that could have been considered a laugh. Her fur ruffled, becoming human skin, silver and black hair on her head, with the same yellow eyes most wolves had. I glared at Eve, but I appreciated her weekly visits. Her cubs approached me, sniffing. I lowered my head, and the smaller one ran to hide behind his mother.

"Sorry," she said, not sounding sorry at all. "I looked for you by the river, and then your howl gave away your location." She grabbed one of the many blankets scattered around our grounds, shaking it off, before wrapping it around herself. With my fur, I didn't feel the cold as she would in her human shape.

I remained in wolf form, eager to return to my hunt. Maybe the rabbit was still around somewhere. I wasn't ready to shift. More comfortable as a wolf, I rarely took human form any more. The smaller cub snuggled against her, while the larger, braver one followed a scent. When he got too far away, Eve growled, and he came running back, with a growl of his own.

"I'm teaching them to hunt," she said, gazing at the two cubs. "Their first time outside the den. They did well for their first hunt."

I lay down beside Eve and rested my head on my paws. Together we watched as the two cubs pounced on each other, play-fighting and growling. Eve's hand ran over my back.

"Parker spoke with your father," Eve said, continuing the motion. "Your uncle was in the meeting too."

I huffed and closed my eyes. Her fingers in my fur relaxed me. I whined with contentment as she scratched the top of my head. My tail thumped on the ground. I let the joy of the moment push away what she'd told me. There was only one reason Parker would speak to my father and the alpha. I let her continue her one-sided conversation.

"Parker is ambitious," Eve said. "He will not be swayed to give up his pursuit of you. You're the one he set his eyes on, and eventually he's going to try to mark you. He believes you are his mate."

I growled, hoping she'd drop the subject, keeping my eyes on the cubs.

Eve sighed. "I know you'd rather avoid talking about this. The pack needs future generations to survive. Wolves are usually paired off long before your age. The alpha has been lenient because he's your uncle. They're really hoping you find a mate tomorrow night."

Tomorrow night? My ears twitched, and I peered up at her.

"Please talk to me, Jewel." Her tone indicated she was hurt by my refusal to speak. "When was the last time you shifted?"

I reflected on her question. Six months. Before that, a year, maybe two. I'd attended pairing ceremonies, only to hide from the hunt. Eve had told me what it felt like when bonded with her mate. Falling in love, and knowing that the Wolf Goddess blessed the union, terrified me beyond any fear I'd ever experienced. To have someone mark me, and to complete the mating bond, I'd be accepting the Goddess's blessing. There were no Silver Moon wolves that I felt that with. So my mate was in another pack.

I rose from my crouch and let the wolf recede. My body tingled as I shifted. Fur became smooth, pale skin, and my paws became hands and feet, my muzzle shrinking into my face, my ears and eyes moving. Eve held up part of the blanket.

"I had hoped he'd give up by now," I said. The sensation of speaking had become strange, unfamiliar. "We're not mates; I don't know why he thinks we are. He can't force what does not exist. I hope he doesn't try to convince my uncle to let him claim or mark me."

Eve gave me a tight smile. "I think that, to Parker, it's more about you being the niece of the alpha, though; so, be careful."

I sighed. "Parker already tried to mark me," I admitted. "The night of my eighteenth birthday. I returned to my wolf, and I ran." I'd given myself to my wolf, rarely returning to human form ever since. The Wilds had become my family.

Eve laughed. "No wonder he's obsessed with you. That age-old wanting what he can't have." She glanced at me. "That's why you joined the Wilds? I had no idea, I'm sorry. Your mate is yet to find you. How will he find you if you are hidden from him?"

The cubs raced around us in circles, one chasing the other, and then swapping. I laughed.

"If there is a wolf that the Goddess has chosen for me, he, or she I guess, will find their way to me, no matter where I am," I said. I hoped the Goddess understood that I just wanted to run, and hunt, and howl.

"Oh, that reminds me!" She turned more serious eyes to me. "Your uncle has invited wolves from other towns to a pairing ceremony. Shadow, Black Rose, Crimson Moon, and Dark Moon packs will all be here. They arrive tomorrow, in time for the full moon."

Great, the mating hunt. Another night I'd have to make an appearance. I'd leave the moment I could. We hadn't had one for a year or so, so it should be no surprise that we were hosting one. I wouldn't let anyone hunt me in the hopes of marking me. It seemed ridiculous that my uncle would go to so much trouble to reach out to packs of other towns, yet avoid the pack right here. The Midnight pack. Something had happened generations before, to cause a rift between our packs. I still had no idea what had caused it, though. I'd never seen any of them, never having any need to leave Silver Moon's territory. My cousin, Tyler, took any opportunity he could to antagonise them, in the hopes someone would initiate a fight. As the next alpha in line, any attack would be a challenge. He and his betas would have no choice but to respond.

"You never know who you'll meet at these events. You might get those fireworks you want to avoid so much. If Parker doesn't get to you first," Eve said.

I stood, uncomfortable at the talk of Parker, the blanket falling from my shoulders.

"Oh, we're done," I said, shifting again.

"Sorry, Jewel," she said. "I went too far." She folded up the blanket. "Ok, let's run," she said. "I've put you in a mood, and I'd rather not be the cause of that scowl of yours."

She quickly shifted, and with her cubs following, we bounded through the trees. Snow crunched under our paws as we wandered aimlessly. Howls filled the air as we neared the village. Wolves of the pack were returning. I didn't even know they'd gone. Instinct told me to lay low, rather than reveal myself, and Eve crouched beside me, watching from our hiding place as wolves who were part of Tyler's entourage shifted to human. She put her paw on one of her cubs, a signal to be quiet. The other one looked up at me with curiosity in his eyes.

"He's pissed," Jackson said. "They really fucked up his car."

"Chances are, he probably did something first," Fletcher laughed. "I mean, they wrote 'dick.'"

All eyes turned to him and he shrugged.

"What did you see?" Tyler's beta captain, Bryce, asked.

Jackson grinned around at the group. "The fight is all anyone's talking about over there. The alpha's muscle have closed in. Roman's nowhere to be seen. I heard his howls, though, so he's in wolf form. One of his betas was hurt, thanks to yours truly."

"It's likely Roman will just smile and talk of peace," Fletcher added.

"He's still without a mate, so until he succeeds, he can talk of peace all he wants," Bryce said.

They all laughed, clearly mocking whoever they were talking about. *Fight?* Probably just Tyler baring his canines again. I loved my cousin, but his hotheadedness was going to start a war with the Midnight Pack. The cubs grew bored and wandered away. Eve and I turned away from the meeting, following.

We approached houses, the lights glinting against the dark night. Eve whined as she turned to leave. She was asking me to stay. Houses were reserved for those with families. Cubs were protected and warm until they reached an age at which they could run free with the pack. I should have had a home within our little village. Instead, I lived in the forest, running with the Wilds. I was content with my life; the village wasn't for me.

I watched Eve and her cubs make their way home, and turned, running back to the place in which I was happiest. The haunting sounds of howls split the night. The other wolves who, like me, chose to live wild. I followed their howls, answering with my own. I was hungry, and they were going hunting.

Chapter 4

ROMAN

I ran to clear my mind. Deeper in the forest, Wilds howled to each other. A couple of she-wolves from the pack ran with me. Always surrounded by those hoping that the Wolf Goddess would choose them for my mate, I was used to it. I leapt towards them playfully, hoping to lift my mood. They took joy in my attention, and I loved the company.

One nuzzled at me, an offer of sympathy after Tobias's injuries became well known amongst the pack. We ran until we reached the base of the snow-capped mountains. Mason's howl echoed through the forest. It was time to return, to find out what my parents would ask of me for letting Tyler provoke me. I was also keen to check on Tobias, so I made my way back to the alpha house.

I waited outside as Mason spoke to pack members about Tobias.

"He's okay; he's been instructed to rest while he heals." Mason caught sight of me and made his way over.

Solstice's voice inside the house informed me of her presence, as she spoke in a low voice. I caught the familiar vampire scent. Spencer had also been here. Gideon and Bennett joined me, lying down beside me.

Mason approached, a glint of mischief in his eyes. I watched him from my crouched position. Gideon and Bennett turned their heads to meet my eyes. Gideon squinted, his ears twitching. Wolves don't have the same expressions humans do, but it was clear they'd noticed, too. Mason was up to something.

He had a heavy jacket and boots on, with a blanket and boots in his hands for me.

"Tobias is okay," Mason reassured us. "He has been ordered to remain human as he heals, so he doesn't tear his stitches. Sienna and Addison are making a fuss over him, so he's living it up."

I relaxed my mouth to show a grin. Mason lowered himself to one knee in front of me. His eyes lost their mischief. "I told you not to get involved, Roman. The alphas are waiting to speak to you."

Oh, fuck. I shifted, and pulled on the boots as Mason wrapped the blanket around me. I took a deep breath and made my way to the house. If one could call it that. Built to house not just my parents, and their betas, but any visiting alphas, it was more like a mansion. Underneath was a den, in which I had been raised, alongside Bennett, Mason, Gideon, and Tobias. All children of my parents' betas, and I had seen no one better to be my own.

Before I entered the house, I glanced back at Mason. Gideon and Bennett remained at his side. I walked through the doors.

"We'll need to do something to cheer him up when he comes home. I actually have an idea," Mason said to the others.

I closed the doors as he walked back to our house with Gideon and Bennett.

"We're in here, son." My dad's voice came from the living room.

I put on my best smile, and I walked in. They were seated in their chairs, so I sat on the couch opposite them.

"You let Tyler provoke you," Mum said, her voice stern.

I bowed my head in shame. "I know," I acknowledged. "I should have listened to Mason. I just lost my temper that he was challenging us on *our* territory. His betas attacked my betas, and I couldn't watch th-."

Mum held a hand up, and I stopped talking. "You cannot have a temper," she reminded me. "Not when you're alpha. Wolves will look to you for leadership. What you did today is not leadership."

My smile slipped. "I'm sorry," I said. "I was just thinking of protecting the pack, my betas. Our territory. Isn't that also what alphas do?"

My dad leaned forward, elbows on his legs and hands

together. "Roman, they're your betas. They took an oath to protect you. That's what they were doing."

Mum nodded. "We heard what Tyler said to you. You were the target today. You proved to him that he can provoke you. That will lead to more attacks." She met my eyes. "For the future of our pack, you cannot risk yourself."

"Tyler has no mate, and he cannot lead his pack until he has his co-alpha. He cannot claim the territory of another pack," Dad pointed out. "Neither can you submit your territory to him until you are alpha. He was purely provoking you, and you played into his paws."

"You've never lost your temper before," Mum observed. "Why today?"

"I suppose what he did to the ute set me off," I admitted. "But you're right. I can be better, I promise."

"We know you can, honey," Mum smiled. "We've seen what kind of alpha you'll be. You've proven yourself worthy of the title. You've shown your capacity, especially last week with the storm. You made sure that all cubs were safe, and you reassured the Wilds. We were incredibly proud of you."

Flooded with warmth, and overwhelmed by a mixture of emotions, I couldn't hold back my joyful grin.

"We know we've done a good job raising you to be the next alpha of the Midnight Pack," she added. "We trust that the pack will be in good hands when we step down. I hope when the packs arrive for the pairing ceremony in spring, that your mate will be among them. We're ready for you to accept your birthright. You're old enough to bear that."

Overwhelmed by the surge of emotion, I nodded. "I hope so too," I agreed. "I know that she will be strong enough to lead with me." I burst with pride at their words.

"But we need this to be a lesson that you remember." Dad ran his hand over his face. It was his 'I really don't want to do this' expression. "You were always difficult to punish as a cub; you always took it as a game. But this one is a fair and just punishment."

My joy faded. I'd forgotten that's why I was in here.

"You are bound to human form for the next three days," Mum said. "No wolf."

The words echoed in my mind, my stomach churning. I could not have guessed they'd set such a harsh punishment. "No wolf? But I'm supposed to lead the full moon hunt tomorrow night," I argued. I'd been looking forward to this. It was the last full moon before the snow would start to melt, to give way to spring.

"I'll be leading it in your place." Dad was firm. "Now go see Tobias. He's been waiting for you."

They left no room for argument. I walked from the living room, my jaw clenched, wishing I had listened to Mason. Tobias's whimpers and two female voices drifted from a room in the back of the house that was often used for injured wolves. Solstice approached me. She had silver dreads, and was of mixed African heritage, with light brown skin. Her eyes were blue, and she always had the scent of burning candles and earth. While appearing only in her thirties, she'd once told me she was over a thousand years old.

"Hi, Roman," she smiled at me. "He was lucky today. He's not going to be very responsive right now. He was scratching at the stitches, so I gave him something to stop him. Gideon was here earlier, and I made him leave, Sienna and Addison just arrived. They're keeping him calm, but I'm going to put a stop to visiting hours soon. He needs his rest. He's still awake, but he's a little drowsy."

I peered through the door. Tobias was awake, his eyes moved to meet mine, but when he tried to lift his head, he gave up, and he groaned at me. Sienna and Addison lay next to him on the bed. I walked in.

"Solstice should have put a cone on you," I joked as I sat down in the chair next to the bed. I gave him the once-over. "Look at you!" I said. "Spoilt with two women curling up next to you!"

His eyes lit up, but when he smiled, saliva pooled at the corner of his mouth.

"Bro, you're drooling!" I pointed out, smirking at him.

"Let me help!" Sienna moved her hand, wiping away the spit.

"You're totally milking this, aren't you?" I asked, smirking down at him.

He whined at me, but the cheeky glint in his eyes indicated that I was right.

"We're both going to miss the full moon hunt," I lamented with a heavy sigh. "My punishment for not listening to Mason." I rolled my eyes. "Don't tell him I said that. He'll rub it in. But when you're up and walking around again, we'll go running. Maybe Sienna and Addison will join us."

Joy crossed the faces of the two she-wolves by his side, as if they'd been chosen for some great reward.

"Look after him, ladies," I said. "I know he'll appreciate it. I'm glad someone's here to keep him company." I jerked my head towards the door. "Solstice will probably kick you out soon, though."

If I hadn't been told 'no wolf', I would have stayed with him myself. But I needed to be moving, and I wanted to go for a ride on my motorbike.

"Sure, Roman," Addison agreed. "I'm sorry all this happened."

She climbed off the bed and wrapped her arms around me in a hug . She was very affectionate, so I embraced her.

I gave her a warm smile when she stepped back. "Don't let him feel sorry for himself," I said.

I left the room and grinned at Solstice. "He's in good hands," I commented. "Can you let them stay for a while?"

"I suppose I can for another hour." Her eyes widened as she studied me.

"What? Do I have food in my teeth?" I asked.

Solstice grabbed my jaw, pulling me down. She peered into my eyes.

"Solstice? What are you doing?" I asked. "If you want me to kiss you, you only need to ask."

She scoffed. "Hate to break it to you, young alpha, but your beta beats you there."

"Oh really?" I grinned at her. "Which one?"

I had a feeling she was talking about Mason.

Instead of answering, her eyes bored into mine again. "Your lips are destined for another. She will not enjoy my scent on you." She winked at me.

My heart skipped a beat. "Wait, have you seen…"

Solstice had the ability to see glimpses of someone's fate. We knew Magic Wielders often held such gifts. Hers had not gone unnoticed by the pack.

She let me go, but I grabbed her arm. "Please, if you've seen something, tell me."

She removed my hand. "Knowing one's fate isn't always a good thing, Roman. Just trust in your Goddess," she instructed.

I stared at her, and she sighed. "Don't look at me with those puppy eyes."

"What did you see?" I asked again, keeping my voice light.

"Please, Solstice."

"Pain and tragedy," she admitted with a heavy voice. "Find the light of the moon in the darkest night. Don't lose yourself. This will be what defines you as an alpha. Your pack will follow you, no matter what happens. You've already proven yourself to them."

She walked away, leaving me stunned. I wanted to follow her, to ask more, but she had said as much as she was going to. I left the house, and her words followed me.

No wolf. It was the worst punishment to place on a wolf, and I'd be clawing at the walls before long. Especially with the full moon. Outside, wolves waited for me. They lowered their heads in respect. I let them approach me.

Without my fur, the cold stung, my hands were numb, and I exhaled white breath. My house was right next door. Necessary, so I was close for alpha business.

Mason, Gideon, and Bennett were sitting in the lounge, fully dressed, feet up on the coffee table, watching TV. Mason held a bag of chips, grabbing a handful, which he pushed into his mouth. I grabbed the bag from him, helping myself before handing the bag back to him.

"Who's up for a ride?" I grinned at Mason, already knowing the answer.

Gideon and Bennett cheered.

"Keen as!" Mason said, standing up. "No wolf?"

"No wolf," I confirmed.

"I saw Spencer when I was at the alpha house," Mason said.

"I know you're up to something. Spit it out," I ordered.

"He's just come from Silver Moon territory. They are holding a pairing ceremony. Out-of-town wolves are arriving in the morning. My guess is, it'll be the Shadow, Black Rose, Crimson

Moon, and Dark Moon packs."

Those packs were the most logical. But they were the very same packs we had invited for the spring.

"There will be so many wolves here," I gushed. "It would be so funny if we went and found our mates there!"

Mason winked. "Then let's go, crash their ceremony!" He beamed.

I laughed, until I realised he was serious. I winced. "Why do I feel like this is another case of Mason getting Roman into trouble?" I asked.

"Because that's all he does!" Bennett pointed out. "Like the time he took you to that concert, and you got kicked out because you didn't have tickets. They wanted to call your parents."

I chuckled.

Gideon grinned. "Oh! What about when he told that big guy that you were an alpha and could kick his ass?"

I winced. "I'd never been in a bar fight before, I didn't know humans didn't have the strength and speed we do."

Mason shrugged. "Hey, I tried to keep you out of trouble today, and you didn't listen, so that one's on you. Anyway, what if you don't go, and you miss out on meeting that wolf you want to keep warm through the night? You go, and you find the one wolf who can't resist your charm, and the hopeless romantic that you are. Quote poetry to her or something."

"Quote poetry?" I couldn't hold back the laughter. "Are you sure you're not just looking for trouble?"

"He wants to go," Gideon remarked to the others. "He's just trying to be all reasonable alpha Roman right now. Let the romantic Roman out, so we can go play."

"You'll never find her if you don't take the risks," Mason

added.

A cold feeling passed through me as Solstice's words played themselves over in my head. By going, would I be avoiding tragedy, or heading towards it? I shrugged it off, my betas all watching me. Mason made sense. I would never find my co-alpha if I didn't seek her out. I gave a slow smile.

"Yes!" Mason fist-pumped the air. "They won't even know we're there!"

"Well what are you all sitting around for?" I asked, chuckling. "Are we going for a ride, or what?"

Gideon and Bennett ran towards their bedrooms. Mason remained, watching me. "You're still not convinced, are you?" he asked.

I flashed my biggest smile at him. "You're right. We should go. We're a wolf down if something goes awry, though."

"You're worried about being caught, aren't you?" he pushed.

"I worry about how Tyler would react to us being on their territory in a ceremony they've organised and clearly not invited us to," I admitted. "He knows our scent, and we don't have the backup of the pack."

"Then put your worries aside!" He grinned at me. "He won't recognise our scent."

I stared at him in silence. "It's a bit hard to hide our scent from another wolf," I said.

Finally, he stood up. "Leave that to me!"

Chapter 5

ROMAN

My wolf became restless, and I feared my control slipping when the moon rose. The urge to shift rumbled through me. I yearned to run, to howl. Suppressing my wolf, I spent the day riding with my betas, talking to the pack, and checking in on Tobias. Gideon spent as much time as he could by Tobias's side.

"Maybe the night of a full moon when I'm forbidden to shift isn't the best time to be going into enemy territory," I told Mason. "My wolf already wants to push through."

"Look at him, trying to reason with me," Mason laughed. "Rome, let's just have some fun."

He had a point, and I couldn't hold back a smile. Pairing ceremonies were huge events, and I couldn't deny that going to one did fill me with hope. It wasn't just the possibility of finding a mate, it was the energy, and the social aspect. I just needed to stay off Tyler's radar.

"There he is!" Bennett said, eyes gleaming with mischief. "He's so keen!"

Mason grasped my shoulder. "He's just trying to be the alpha, all responsible and shit. He wants to go as much as the rest of us."

"'*He*' is right here," I muttered. "Stop talking about him —me — as if I'm not."

My betas laughed.

"Okay, you win, I wouldn't mind going," I admitted.

Mason fist-pumped the air. "Yes! That's my alpha wolf!"

I rolled my eyes and walked to my bedroom.

Mason stood in the doorway as I reached for my jacket. Gideon and Bennett appeared in the doorway behind Mason.

"So, what's your plan to cover our scent?" I reminded Mason.

Mason's grin only widened. "Wait here!" He left my room, only to return a minute later with a spray bottle in hand.

"What's that?" I asked.

"Lift your arms," he said.

I did as he asked, and he sprayed my chest and torso.

I sneezed and gagged. "Oh, what *is* that?" I asked, louder. It was pungent, and my wolf disliked it too. I growled. I looked down at my tee-shirt. "Oh I'm going to need to burn this!"

Bennett covered his mouth with a hand. "It smells like something died."

"Something Solstice made up for me," Mason said as he sprayed Gideon. "In half an hour, it won't be so strong, but it will cover our scent."

Bennett backed up. "Uh-uh. You're not spraying me with that shit."

"Then you're staying behind," I said, laughing. I couldn't blame him. "I have to get sprayed; so do you."

Bennett growled, but let Mason spray him.

Once we were all smelling like rotting carcass, Mason led us to the carport, where our Hondas and my ute were parked. I pulled on my jacket and grabbed my helmet off my seat.

"It's a pity Tobias is missing out on this," Gideon commented. "He'll be bummed."

"Yeah, I'm sure he wants to smell like a skunk with the rest of us," Bennett said, pulling on his helmet.

I pushed at him. "Do you even know what skunk smells like?"

"No, but I imagine it smells as bad as this," Bennett said, his voice muffled.

Finally, we climbed on the bikes, started the engines, and left through the roller door. As soon as we were on the road, members of my pack bounded after us. I stopped the bike. A wolf, Yasmin, approached, sniffing at the air. Her eyes widened in shock, and she sneezed, shaking her head.

"I know, I stink," I said in agreement and addressed the pack. "Who's excited for the full moon hunt tonight?"

The wolves let loose a howl, long and joyful. I climbed off

my bike, and I knelt before them, lifting my visor. "I was supposed to lead it, but after what happened yesterday, I'm prohibited from shifting. So I expect you all to tell me all about it tomorrow morning!" I turned my focus to Iris and Lukas. "How are the cubs? Are you taking them tonight?"

Lukas let his mouth drop into a smile and dipped his head enough to be a nod.

"Their first hunt!" I grinned at him. "That's so cool. I really wish I could see that. It won't be long before they're shifting and getting into trouble. Like their cousin." I glanced back at Mason, smirking at him. I rose to my feet and pointed to my bike. "Can you keep up?" I asked the crowd around me. A couple of wolves leapt into the air, while others gave me their widest wolfish grins. "To the gates," I said and slammed down my visor, returning to my bike.

Natural wolves would not have been able to keep up. But we had the added advantage of supernatural speed and strength, a gift from the Goddess. They ran beside our bikes without effort. We passed through the gates, wolves behind us howling.

"You were so born for this!" Mason stated through his helmet. "They love it when you ride."

"They love everything you do," Gideon added. "You've always got time to listen to the pack, to relate to them."

"Being their alpha is as natural as breathing for you," Bennett agreed. "You know everyone's names, and you support the cubs through their first shift. You really will make an incredible alpha, cuz."

A warm sensation unfurled in my chest. It meant a lot for my betas to say that. "Let's go," I said. "We have a party to crash."

It didn't take long to get to the Silver Moon lands. Their celebration was under way. Music, food, drink. The smell of cooked meat made me heave. Some wolves were known to be okay with it. But I could never stomach anything not freshly killed. Even when I went into town, the scent of barbecues or cooked steaks had been overpowering.

"I hope any potential mates never try to bring that habit into the house," Mason declared. "We'd never get rid of the smell."

We were mostly ignored by everyone. One wolf who walked too close glanced up at me.

"Yeah, I'd be hiding my face if I smelt like that too," he said. "You roll in your dinner or something?"

He was not a wolf I knew. "Or something," I agreed.

I scanned the crowd, relieved that there was no sign of Tyler. *Yet.* My eyes paused on every wolf, studying their faces. Many of these wolves were supposed to be attending our ceremony in spring, and I wasn't feeling anything about them. Mum had told me often it was skin-on-skin contact that awoke the bond. I fidgeted with my gloves and gave up on the wolves around me.

With a sigh, I turned around, my gaze stopping on a dark-haired woman standing at the edge of the crowd. She wore only gumboots, a blanket wrapped around her. My wolf howled, and I held back the urge to do the same. I couldn't look away. She was a beauty, but that wasn't what drew my attention. A glint within her eyes hinted that there was a wild side to her. The way she stayed back, and wasn't in clothes like everyone else, was another indication. Her head jerked, and she took a step back as someone wandered too close. *Is she a Wild?* Surely not; they didn't take human form again. *Who brought a Wild?*

Warmth engulfed my heart, and again I wanted to howl. But more than that, the urge to shift washed over me, the desire to give chase.

"Oh, fuck," I muttered, my voice guttural as the wolf spoke through me. "Mine."

My betas barely noticed, looking around at the visiting wolves.

"Excuse me," Mason said, lifting his visor. "I have wolves to talk to!" His voice dropped as he glanced around, eyes lighting up with yearning.

Whether Mason found his mate or not, he'd likely find a wolf to keep him warm through the night. He had an energy that drew people to him, made them smile. His affection for those around him shone through, and he had once told me he cared little about gender. His claims that what's on the inside meant more to him made sense.

I gravitated towards females, and had my nights with she-wolves, while Mason didn't care. He took both. Our Goddess, therefore wolves, didn't discriminate against unions the way humans were known to. That level of hatred was a human ideology that no wolf understood. Every wolf had a right to love who they wanted, to be themselves without judgement. The humans' dislike of anyone different was the very reason we feared being discovered.

The Goddess was known to bless couples regardless of their gender. Much to our delight, Gideon and Tobias had formed their mate bond a couple of years before, but still accepted females into their beds. A way for same-sex mates to continue their line was to find a surrogate. Several females of our pack hoped to fulfil that role.

Mason left us, and it wasn't long before Bennett and Gideon wandered off. They said something as they left, but I barely noticed, unable to look away from the dark-haired she-wolf, enraptured by her presence. Was I just being hopeful, or was there something nudging me towards the wild-looking wolf? My mouth was dry, my wolf begging to hunt her, and I couldn't move, couldn't look away. As she took in her surroundings, her gaze paused on me for a second. Of course, she wouldn't see that I was staring at her through my visor.

Tyler's voice drew my attention away from her for a split second. He was laughing with his betas. When I looked back towards the woman, she was gone. I walked towards where I'd seen her, and lifted my visor slightly. I caught a fresh scent that reminded me of a spring morning after fresh rain. Convinced it had to be her, I followed the trail.

Cubs ran past me, growling at each other, until one tackled the other. It would be a few years before they'd make their first shift to human, so until then, they were pure wolf. Many were given shelter in dens dug beneath houses during winter. We generally spent most of our lives the way natural wolves did. Not that I'd seen a natural wolf. I walked away from the music and the dancing crowd, following the scent. My senses took me into the forest, and small, light bootprints showed me the way.

I came to a stop when I walked into a clearing, a large river in front of me. A wooden bridge lay across the river, and I walked over it, until I saw her. She had taken a seat at the water's edge, gazing into the pool. I leaned against the railing, just watching her. Waves of black hair cascaded down her back, and I imagined lifting it up and sinking my canines into the nape of her neck, victorious after chasing her. The vision brought my cock to attention, shifting uncomfortably against my jeans. The very sight of her brought a rush of warmth and need I had never felt with such an intensity. I struggled to hold my wolf back, and a sound halfway between a growl and a groan escaped my lips.

She lifted her head, her eyes on me in an instant. My heart stopped at the icy glare she gave me.

"Did you follow me?" she accused, rising to her feet.

"Forgive me," I pleaded, fighting back the need to flee. Her unwelcoming expression stung. "I could not look away from you. I didn't mean to creep you out. I am not accustomed to such wild beauty, and I wanted to catch a glimpse of you again. I did not expect your voice to be as enchanting as you." The words that came from me surprised me. I never spoke in such a way. But I found myself wanting to charm her, hoping my words would soften her hard stare.

She walked towards the end of the bridge. "Your words are romantic. But you hide behind a shield." She sniffed the air. "Your scent is a little strange. Are you a wolf?"

I grinned, even though she couldn't see it. "Think of this as my armour, as I disguise myself from a threat."

She took a step onto the bridge, and I wanted to close the distance. The wild glint was still there, and I held myself still. If she was wild, even partially, I had to let her come to me. "I at least deserve to see who watches me, while concealing himself from me. Let me look upon your face."

My wolf responded to her words, increasing my struggle to hold still as she advanced on me.

"If you want that, then you'll have to earn it," I told her.

She was only a few metres away from me, and she stopped. "Earn it?" she asked. "Why shouldn't I have the right to see the face of a stalker?"

"Stalker?" I asked. "More of an admirer." I gave in to my yearning, and stepped forward. She held onto the blanket, as she studied me. I lifted a hand, caressing her cheek. "Will you let me kiss you if I give you what you want?"

She laughed. "The hunt hasn't started yet," she said. "Your attempts to chase me are premature. Maybe you'll find more wolves wanting to be chased with the party."

She didn't want me there. I fought back the urge to whimper, winded.

"Why do I feel like you came here to avoid the hunt?" I asked.

She smiled. "Because I did."

Despite her possible rejection, she wasn't moving away.

"If you want to sit quietly by the river, I can sit with you," I offered, partially relaxing. "Keep any other wolves at bay."

Her hands came up, the blanket falling to the ground. Before I could stop her, she lifted my helmet from my head.

Chapter 6

JEWEL

The helmet came off. His black hair reached the nape of his neck. He was unshaven, with a narrow face, and evidence of spending time in the sun. I was taken aback, not sure what I'd been expecting. His lips curved into a smile, and our eyes locked. There was a tenderness in his expression, and a sheer joy as he gazed at me. Relieved to find yellow eyes staring into mine, I recognised the telltale silver ring on the outside of his yellow iris. *Alpha.* He was the next in line to rule a pack.

There was a spark within him that I recognised. His wolf was powerful, whispering to mine. My wolf wasn't afraid of him, instead, wanting to clamp her jaws on his neck or shoulder. He lifted a hand, his thumb touching my lip, his breathing hitched.

Mine. My wolf claimed him, her silent voice threatening to break through my lips. Surprised by my own reaction to him, wolf and body, I felt emboldened. My urge to flee from this stranger–who prompted a rush of desire to surge through me–dissipated. I considered licking him.

"I would not have known you were a wolf by your scent alone," I said, suppressing my urges. "But there is no way to hide what you are with those eyes."

His smile widened, white teeth on display. Top and bottom canines showed his wolf close to the surface. I licked my lips, heat trickling through my muscles. He licked his own lips, eyes dropping to my mouth.

"Can I kiss you?" he asked. His voice was rich, deep, rumbling from him. My wolf stretched out, wanting to touch him.

He lowered his head and paused, waiting, his eyes on mine.

"You're a gentleman," I laughed. "But why do you hesitate? Did you follow me for a kiss, or to stare at me?"

He chuckled. "I followed a flower, only to find someone worth a chase. I'm in the presence of a wild beauty, and I am afraid of you fleeing like a dream."

I melted, his words flowing from him, his eyes holding me captive.

"Are you always this way with your words?" I murmured,

afraid to give in to the desire blazing deep within me. "They make my heart soar and sink at the same time. Do you charm me with your flattering tongue that will disappoint me when you have what you want?"

He chuckled. "My friends tell me I'm a hopeless romantic. But I stand behind my words. Let my kiss answer all the questions your heart holds," he whispered. With a finger under my chin, he tilted my head, our lips almost touching. "If you like the flattery of my tongue, I can show you what else it can do."

A wicked gleam in his eyes sent fresh waves of heat. He was close enough to kiss me, but still he waited.

"What are you waiting for?" I panted. "Is your wolf timid?"

"My wolf rejoices in your presence, and howls to make you mine." He quietly imitated a howl. "To give chase, until you either fight me or let me catch you. To bite that spot that will show the world that you are taken. If your wolf isn't too wild to allow it. Then under the stars, we shall hunt."

He'd recognised the wild nature in me, something that seemed to escape the attention of wolves in my own pack. Only a minute with me and he was respecting my wolf's skittishness. His offer for us to hunt *together* only intrigued me more. Who was this wolf, that he would not offer to hunt *for* me? Every wolf I knew wanted to show me what they could provide for me.

Warm breath caressed my lips. I closed the space, hungry to know him, hoping that this prince of charm was not about to break me.

The kiss filled me with joy, leaving me wanting more. My wolf inside howled to be let out. She wanted to run with this hot stranger, with his honeyed words that melted me. Still holding his helmet, I locked my arms behind his neck. Cold air caressed my skin, but I was enveloped by warmth when his arms wrapped around my bare back, pulling me in tight against him. One gloved hand slid up. In his embrace, I was home. His tongue massaged mine, unrelenting, his kiss gentle. I could feel that he was holding himself back. Warmth unfurled like a waking rose. My wolf was as taken by this stranger as I was.

We both ended the kiss with reluctance, catching our breath. My wolf was so close to the surface, I struggled to hold back the shift. I wasn't sure I wanted to anyway. If I shifted, he'd have no choice but to do so as well. I'd give him a chase, all right. I'd make him work for it. I knew this land, and while he was looking for me, I could turn everything around and mark *him*. I grinned at the thought.

His arms were strong, and his warmth against my body left me panting with need. I yearned to tear his clothes off. "Your wolf calls to me," I murmured. "He wants to give chase."

Amusement sparked in his eyes. "Perhaps." He pulled his gloves off, his warm hands on my skin. His lips were equally warm as they found mine again. I soared through our second kiss. My skin blazed where he touched me, my human body reacting. I was wet, and he could probably smell it.

"If you're not careful, my wolf will come out," I whispered.

"Would that be so bad?" he asked. He leaned forward to whisper in my ear. "Your wolf wants to be chased. Let her out to play?"

I whimpered. "Let yours out first."

Frustration then clouded his face. "I'm under restriction, to deny my wolf for three days. So I'll have to chase you in this form."

A punishment. I licked his cheek, my wolf ready to break through. Black fur rippled across my skin, the shiver down my spine indicating I was about to lose control. "Who from your pack will know if we slip into the forest where no one can see us?" My voice had changed tone, as my wolf and I spoke together. I wasn't sure why I was pushing him to disobey his alpha's orders. Whatever the reason for his restriction, I should respect the demands of another pack's alpha.

His eyes betrayed his struggle. He was a wolf who obeyed orders, but he wanted to give in. He growled low in his throat, his eyes showing a savageness, untamed and wild. It filled me with glee. His eyes widened, his own need and the strength of the full moon becoming too much for him. Fur rippled across his face.

"Oh, fuck," he grunted, and pulled off his jacket, revealing tattooed, muscular arms. Oh, Goddess, this really was about to happen. I was about to let someone chase me. Next, he tore his tee-shirt in two. "Run!" His tattooed abs and chest mesmerised me. "I mean it. You need to run *now.*" His tone was commanding, and my wolf wanted to obey.

His wolf was doing the talking. Something that only happened in that moment before a shift, when we were no longer separate. When we became one and took our natural form. Black fur rippled across his skin and faded again. He really was struggling to hold his wolf back. I took a step back from him as he kicked off his boots.

"Fuck," he cursed as he struggled with his jeans. His fingers had become claws. He looked up at me again. I swear his black hair looked longer. "What are you waiting for? I said, *runnnn.*" His words ended on a deep animalistic growl that turned my insides to jelly.

A shiver ripped through me. It was as if his wolf was speaking directly to mine. But there was something deeper. His words were commanding, making them hard to resist. His alpha spark. To have drawn the attention of a future alpha made me want to tear his clothes off with my teeth. My wolf agreed. The yearning and desire that filled me with heat born from his growls only made me more excited for what was about to take place.

I dropped the blanket, kicking off my own boots, and the shift took me. My own fur rippled across my skin, my face changing shape, canines lengthening, claws ripping through my fingers.

A growl echoed through me. He'd already shifted, a second before I did. His wolf advanced on me slowly, lowering his head. When he bared his teeth, I let my mouth fall into a smile, my tail moving side to side of its own free will. I hated pairing ceremonies and mating hunts, but I wanted him to chase me. I'd never needed this like I did then.

I turned and ran further into the forest.

Chapter 7

ROMAN

S he was the one. Through Mason's determination to crash the pairing ceremony, fate had sent me to this Wild wolf, bringing us together. I'd taken part in mating hunts before. However, never had I ever wanted to chase a wolf as much as this one. I didn't know her name, but I would have her. I'd accidentally tapped into my alpha spark when I told her to run, adding a pull to my voice that no wolf could fight. I'd seen surprise within the flare of defiance as she fought against it. I listened to her retreating footsteps and ragged breaths as she bolted.

After giving her a slight head start, I followed, trusting my senses to keep on her tail. Even through her wild look, she'd melted at my words and let me kiss her. Now I had to mark her, and the thrill of the hunt bubbled up. Overflowing with excitement, I sniffed at the ground. She'd come this way! I raised my head and released a long howl. An alert to my betas that I was on the hunt. They would need to witness my victory.

I had broken my alphas' command by shifting. They would learn of this, and I'd face consequences. But I didn't care. I *couldn't* care. I was the wolf, locked onto my target. I ran in the direction she'd gone, deeper into the forest.

Her scent changed, footprints becoming human in the snow. I searched my surroundings. She was trying to throw me off, shifting. Her footprints stopped at a tree, and I searched the top. No sign of her. I sniffed the ground and the bark of the tree. She had climbed. I stretched, standing on my hind legs, leaning against the trunk. Her scent was there, but it didn't go up far. I turned, looking for the tell-tale sign that she hadn't climbed the tree.

Yes! There! Deep prints in the snow. She'd used the tree to boost herself up, leapt away, and the wolf had landed in the snow. I let myself smile. She was making me work for this, making it more than just a chase. Creating gaps in her prints and in her scent trail. The next gap looked like she was digging into her supernatural strength, bounding instead of running. I leapt after her prints.

A howl echoed around me, nearby — in challenge. *Hers?* It echoed, making it difficult to pinpoint where she was. I growled, putting speed into my run. Trees were getting closer together, slowing me down, and I stopped when her trail did. Her scent was completely gone, no prints: foot or paw. I searched the trees, and lowered myself to the ground, trying to find anything that stood out in the snow.

I turned around, not finding any sign of her. A whimper escaped my throat before I could hold it back. It couldn't be over already. Had she given in to the wild nature that I'd seen within her eyes? I howled again, hoping she'd reply. Human laughter. I turned around. She was jump shifting, which would wear her out. I moved towards where I was sure the laughter had come from, aware of everything around me.

The forest here was darker, blocking out the moonlight. If I didn't find her, I didn't know my way out. Not ready to give up, I kept moving. A growl to my right, and a dark shape darted towards me. I turned to brace, but it was too late. She hit me hard, tackling me to the ground. I fought for control, to get her under me, savage growls rising from me. Her own growls matched mine, as she fought just as hard. Her refusal to let me pin her to the ground only added to my determination. I snarled, twisting us around trying to get her throat in my jaws.

Her snarls were menacing, and her eyes showed no humanity. She was all wolf, having given in to that animalistic, instinctual part of herself. *I am an alpha, I will not let her get the best of me!* Our growls and snarls filled the air as we rolled over the snow.

Finally, I gained control of both of us, pinning her beneath me. But before I could mark her, her head darted up, jaw closing over my shoulder. She clamped on, her bite unmovable. Canines pierced my skin, and I yelped.

She had marked me first, taking me completely by surprise. She released me and tilted her head in a way to let me know she was ready for me to mark her. I nudged her, and I licked her muzzle. The place I wanted to bite was the back of her neck. I nipped at her throat, not quite marking her, trying to get to the back of her neck. Her eyes glinted, and she rolled over beneath me.

I bit hard, making sure to pierce her skin under her coat. The mark would show in her human skin, and it would heal, but not completely. We usually healed quickly enough, but marks from our mate never faded. She would bear my mark for the rest of our days, just as I would bear hers.

I released her, easing my weight from her. She climbed to her feet, rubbing her head under my throat. I snapped at her playfully. She was mine, and I was hers. There was no undoing that. She flopped down on her side, waiting for me. I lay down beside her, our bodies pressed together. She licked at my shoulder where she'd bitten me. Her warmth and her very presence made me drowsy. I closed my eyes.

I awoke at the sound of a nearby wolf howling. *Mason!* I lifted my head, whining. I could tell by the tone of his howl that he was still in human form. That meant he had something to say. He howled again. He was warning me of something. I rose to my feet, hesitant to leave her.

"Roman!" Mason called out, his voice almost whispered, urgent. Other voices indicated that Gideon and Bennett were with him.

I shifted back to human, my companion's yellow eyes moving over my body. I smirked down at her. "I have to go," I told her.

She shifted too. "We are yet to hunt together." She stepped forward, reaching for my cock, her eyes on mine. "Or to finish our ceremony. You promised to show me what else you could do with your tongue."

Her bold words and action jolted me. I'd never had a wolf just grab me in this manner. Wolves usually showed me high regard. She'd accepted that I was an alpha, and she had shown herself to be my equal. My breath hitched as I gazed down at her.

"We will," I promised. "Give me three nights, I'll return. We can run, hunt and anything else you want. There's a lot we have to talk about, too."

"That you're an alpha?" she asked. "That I'll be your co-alpha?"

I nodded, and I pulled her to me. My kiss was gentle at first, but it quickly grew rough, demanding. There was a responsibility that came with pairing with me. She reacted not just to my kiss, but to the way our bodies pressed together. I stepped back, my wolf aching to take back control.

"Roman!" Mason called out again. "I know you're here, I can both smell and hear you."

"Mason, relax!" I called out. "Three nights," I whispered. "On the bridge where we first lay eyes upon each other and I was gifted with your voice." Packs usually remained for a week after pairing ceremonies. Especially if a wolf had to leave their territory.

Mason, Gideon, and Bennett approached. Gideon carried my clothes, and Bennett my helmet. Mason's eyes widened as he took in the sight of us, stopping on my shoulder. His mouth fell into a wide grin and he turned his focus to my mate. I lifted her hair and gently pushed at her so she'd turn around. She showed my betas my mark, and I kissed it gently.

A silver wolf darted in, not one I recognised. She shifted

in front of us, barely looking at me. "Jewel, your mother is looking for you. Parker has declared a claim to you, and he is looking to mark you tonight."

I growled at the idea that another would try to lay claim to her. Yet I also marvelled at the beauty of her name. My Jewel. The strange woman looked at me, and she let out a gasp.

Mason pulled me back. "Roman, we *have* to go. Tyler recognised your howl. He's on a warpath."

I let him and the others pull me away. We left Jewel, but I turned, rushing back to the clearing to get another glimpse of her.

"Roman!" There was annoyance in Mason's voice now. "We have to go! What are you doing?"

Another wolf approached Jewel and her friend. This one I knew, and I froze. Arabella Carpenter. Her husband was brother to one of the alphas of the Silver Moons. Her mother? But that meant–*no!* It couldn't be.

"His name is Roman Morrison," Jewel's friend whispered into her ear. "Next alpha in line to the Midnight pack. His pack and ours are enemies."

Jewel met my eyes, a small exhale coming from her, shock filtering through her eyes. The forest around me spun. I had marked and been marked by my enemy.

Chapter 8

ROMAN

Her scent followed me. Jewel. As beautiful as a rose with a wild heart. I wanted to howl her name, tell the world she was mine. Recalling the hunt, and the fight she'd given me, I grinned like an idiot. Her fight had purely been for show. I would have faced more of a challenge if she'd not wanted me to mark her. That she'd marked me first only made her more ideal for the role of my co-alpha. She would be my equal in every way, and I couldn't wait to present her to the pack.

I lost my smile. How would it work with her being part of the Silver Moons? Her pack would never let her join mine, and my alphas would be just as difficult. How had I fallen under the sway of an enemy? My wolf didn't care; he wanted her. She was ours, and that was all that mattered. The revelation of her identity didn't change how I felt about her. Surely we wouldn't have been deemed a match, only for fate to tear us apart?

Wrapped in warmth, I let my betas lead me back to our bikes. I'd found my mate, and I'd marked her. My wolf wanted more, and if I was being honest with myself, I was suppressing the urge to turn around and return to her.

Tyler screamed my name, fury clear in his voice. If he found us, he'd have every right to attack, and we would be outnumbered. Luckily, we'd evaded his betas trying to close in on us. I'd pulled my jeans, boots, and jacket on, tucking my torn tee-shirt through the loops in my jeans. I'd been a little too eager to remove my clothes, and I didn't remember tearing my tee-shirt.

Mason's spray hadn't worn off yet, keeping Tyler from tracking us by scent. As I reached my bike, I sighed.

"Roman has found someone who sends his heart soaring!" Mason commented with laughter. "He sighs, lovesick and full of longing." The others laughed. Mason pulled at the collar of my jacket, exposing Jewel's mark. "He wears her mark. Perhaps he has met his match."

My grin was back in place.

"Lovesick puppy," Mason said.

"He is giddy with love!" Bennett declared. "Wolves have been vying for his attention for years, and he fell for one he'd only just met. The Midnight women will be heartbroken."

I laughed. "They still have a chance with the likes of you, cousin!"

I pulled my helmet on, climbing onto my bike. I paused for a second, listening. Tyler had gone quiet.

"He's shifted to wolf, and he's upwind," Mason advised me, before pulling on his own helmet. "Now is a good time to leave."

"Agreed!" I said, pulling down the visor. I started my bike and eased it into gear. The four of us made our hasty exit.

We were close to the boundary of Silver Moon territory when a howl echoed, closer than I expected. But it wasn't the one I was fearing. Instead of filling me with dread, it set my wolf off. Jewel! My Wild Rose. She had followed us. *Me.* I slowed down, letting my betas gain distance.

She came out of the dark, body low, moving as if she were hunting me. I climbed off my bike and lowered myself to one knee, to her level. I studied her. She was just as stunning in wolf form as she was in human. The wild nature that gleamed from her eyes excited me and my wolf. Who would have thought it would be a Wild who drew me in?

"Why are we from packs fated to hate one another?" I murmured. *Why must the wolf who sings to mine be a Silver Moon?* It hurt that everything about her was perfect for me and I hadn't had her yet. That I might never have her because of who she was.

She took on her human form. Naked, breathtaking. Her black hair flowed down her back. Her yellow eyes focused on me and I rose to my feet.

"You are beautiful, my lady wolf. I had no idea who it was I was marking. If you brought your pack to finish me, let me gaze upon you as I die; I will die a happy wolf," I declared.

"I would no sooner see you die, than grant my own death," she said. "I do not come here for hate. There is enough of that between our packs. I came here for the wolf who marked me, offered me sweet words, and then ran into the night when all I wanted was his warmth. I wish I could change who we were, that we were from any other pack. That you weren't next in line to lead that pack, of all packs. That we could rejoice with our families instead of sharing a shadowed love."

My heart raced. "You said, 'love'?" I stepped forward. "My own thoughts reflect on the word, and I know my heart. To hear you say it gives me hope. I do not want to leave you. I would dream of waking to you beside me. If I never see the light of day again, you are the light of the moon in the darkest night."

Find the light of the moon in the darkest night. Solstice's words! She had seen this.

"Your words send shivers through me, setting me on fire," she whispered. "We were interrupted, and I needed to follow you, to know your kiss once more. So I can take that warmth with me."

I removed my helmet and placed it on my bike, before unzipping my jacket. Cold air brushed against my chest and abs. No more words passed between us as she grabbed the front of my jacket, pulling me towards her. Her heated skin pressed against mine. Our hearts beat in rhythm with one another's, the vibrations drumming through my chest. She gazed up at me, waiting. My hands rested on her hips, before I gave in, sliding them around her back. With our bodies hard against each other, warmth flickered deep within, quickly becoming an all-consuming inferno.

I lowered my head, and her lips parted slightly in response. I wanted to be tender, and I gently licked her soft and warm lips before slipping my tongue past them. My primal nature rose up, the desire to remove my jeans and claim her. My wolf growled, the kiss and her body my sole focus. The world faded and I yearned to take her home, to have her in my arms as we let our urges take us. My cock responded to my desire, making it more difficult to resist her.

The tenderness ceased, our lips locked, the kiss hungry, fiery. She moaned against my mouth. I couldn't get enough of her presence, her skin, her body. I broke the kiss with reluctance, both of us panting.

She leaned into my embrace, resting her head against my chest. "You said we can hunt together in three nights, but I don't think I can wait that long. I want you now," she whispered.

I kissed the top of her head. "Then meet me before sunrise in neutral territory," I murmured. "The point between our territories, in the valley. There is a fork in the river. Hunting there is prime."

She lifted her head, smiling up at me. "You sound like you've hunted there. Risky."

I grinned. "I was once a reckless wolf, thinking it bold to challenge Tyler. But no one will be awake at three in the morning. I will return my bike and wait for the moment my betas fall asleep. We will hunt and run and howl at the moon and all that our heart desires before the harsh light of day brings the truth down around us again."

She kissed me again.

"I don't want to be apart from you," she whispered. "I will count down the seconds until I see you again."

I was just as reluctant to let her leave, afraid that her pack would prevent her from seeing me. If they did, I would cross into their territory to find her. "I will see you at the fork in the river," I promised.

The sound of bikes approaching indicated my betas had turned around for me. I pulled on my helmet.

"You are as hot in leather and that helmet as you are in fur," she said.

"I could live with that," I said with a smile. "Goodnight, sweet Jewel, until the morning."

As I climbed back onto my bike, she took her wolf form again, darting back towards where she had come from.

I couldn't hold back the smile. I would have what I'd thought was beyond my reach. I hoped we'd do more than just hunt. I could show her the cave I'd found when exploring the valley as a teenager.

I'd never felt this way before. I knew the responsibility on my shoulders, and that which I put on anyone I paired with. Many she-wolves had tried hard for my affection, and I'd simply flirted, uncommitted, untouched the way I was with Jewel. I'd never felt such a pull towards any wolf. I knew what this was. A natural occurrence of our people. To be apart from her set off a growing unease. But I would see her again, my beautiful Wild Rose.

Chapter 9

JEWEL

I remained hidden as the wolves hunted each other, seeking mates. Howls filled the air. I recognised Parker's scent, his agonised howl. I lay my head in my paws, staring at the river.

"He's looking for you," Tyler said from behind me.

He sat down on the rocky ground beside me, putting a blanket and boots between us. I shifted, and wrapped the blanket around myself.

"I wanted to make sure you were okay," he said. "We had Midnight wolves invade our territory. One of them, the next alpha in line, I think he was hunting someone. I'd recognise his howl anywhere."

I didn't say anything, afraid of his reaction that the next alpha in line of the Midnight pack had marked me, and I'd marked him. I could still feel it, at the back of my neck, and I resisted the urge to press my fingers over the mostly healed scar.

Tyler glanced at me. "Jewel?"

I smiled. "I'm okay," I said finally. I'd have to tell him eventually. But that could wait until after I'd completed the mating ritual with Roman. "I think a pair found each other." I pointed down-river. "I heard them talking down there. Then mating."

He laughed. "I'm glad we had some success. Bryce found his mate too."

I frowned. "I heard him and the others talking yesterday. You had a fight with the Midnight pack. Did you really go to their territory to attack them?"

"I couldn't help myself. He ruined my car. Clawed the word, 'Dick' into my door, and then shredded the tyre. Then one of them marked his territory on the same tyre last night."

I burst out laughing. Tyler growled, and I only laughed more. "Tyler, you attacked them on their territory because you were upset over your car? Can you blame them for pissing on the damned thing?" I met his eyes. "I know you *and* your ego. Was their damage unprovoked, or did you do something first?"

Tyler rolled his eyes. "I may have clawed his ute first. I

couldn't help myself, I saw it sitting there and–"

"And you lost your shit," I finished for him. "Tyler, shouldn't you have learned to control your temper by now? Is this the kind of alpha you want to be? The pack will need you to be level-headed."

He glared down at me, but his expression softened. The two of us sat in silence for a few minutes. Nearby, more wolves howled.

"You really won't join the hunt?" he asked. "Your mate might be out there."

Oh, believe me, he was. I smiled up at my cousin. "Are you hoping that it's Parker? I think we would have sensed the mate bond by now if it was. I heard he's been talking to your father, and mine. You know we can't force this. Do you want to anger the Goddess?"

He smiled. "I just want to make sure you're happy, provided for. Not just as the next alpha, but as your cousin."

I stood up, his head lifting to meet my eyes. "I am happy," I said. "I don't need to live in a house to be happy. Trust that it will happen naturally, not forced by a hopeful wolf who can't let go of his own ambition. It will happen when it's supposed to." I hated lying to him.

He rose to his feet. "I trust you. It will have to be someone who can accept your wild nature." He laughed. "Maybe he's as wild as you are. Have you felt any draw to the Wilds?"

Now was the time to tell him. I opened my mouth. Taking in his joyful smile as he looked at me, I couldn't do it. His hatred for Roman and the Midnight pack might send him back for another attack. He was already furious that Roman had been on our territory. I wondered if it was more than just his presence, but the fear of a Midnight wolf bonding with a Silver

Moon wolf. I groaned. "Tyler, you have to stop. Maybe focus on finding your own mate, so you can step into being an alpha. Don't worry about me." I shot him a grin. "Maybe she'll help with that hotheadedness of yours. Help you keep it in check."

He hugged me with one arm. "I don't need a mate for that, when my cousin works so hard to do it."

"Who would do that in my place if I were to leave?" I added.

His eyes had the same silver ring around the yellow that Roman's had. One day they'd be silver, and he'd take over as alpha. I worried that he would seek out trouble with the Midnight Pack. Especially once it became known that I was Roman's mate.

"That's something we can address if that ever happens," he commented, standing. "Do you feel like running?"

I laughed. "You ask a question to which you already know the answer."

His eyes dulled, and for a moment I saw all the pressure on him. "I could do with just forgetting about everything for an hour or so," he admitted. "Just give in to the wolf."

"Are your parents upset over what happened?" I pressed.

He nodded. "I'm not supposed to shift. They said I brought shame to the pack, and as always, it took the vampire to calm the situation."

"Yet you're still keen to shift," I said.

He pointed to the full moon "It's inhumane to contain a wolf on such a night," he replied, and he took his jacket off.

Without a word, we shifted and ran side by side.

Chapter 10

ROMAN

“To Roman!” Mason said, holding up a bottle of beer. “Our alpha, about to take on his role.”

We clinked our bottles together. Now that I had found my mate, and marked her, I could feel the increase in strength in my alpha spark. That presence of power within my chest had intensified, unfurling to spread outwards. It wouldn't be long before my parents sensed it too. I hadn't told them yet, as I would also have to tell them I'd disobeyed their orders. But they would soon come to me, to discuss the passing of the spark.

I held up my bottle. "Cheers!" I took a swig of cold beer. "Let's not tell the pack yet."

Mason's head jerked in my direction. "You want to keep a secret from the pack? That is not a good start to your being alpha," he pointed out.

I eyed my beer. "Not for long," I replied. "I just need time. We were interrupted. Give me a couple of days."

Mason's grin widened. "I do believe our alpha has plans to see her again," he said, the others laughing.

"We haven't hunted," I pointed out. "All we did was mark each other and nuzzle. I want her to myself before I present her to the pack." Afraid of how the pack would react to the presence of an enemy, I wanted to hold that off as much as possible. Would this put my leadership into question? Who would take my place if I was to lose my position? I pushed down my rising dread. I didn't want to think of any of that. It would only darken my time with her.

"What's it like?" Mason asked. "To find the one chosen for you?"

I grinned. "It feels like my heart is whole, that I am complete in her presence. I've never known such intense feelings. The moment I laid eyes on her, I knew, and I followed her into the forest in hope to speak with her. To know her, as my heart already knew she was mine."

Mason put his hand on my shoulder. "Tell us how you charmed her. She would not have been able to resist a big, strong alpha." His eyes were filled with amusement.

"My words, and my lips," I declared. "But I hunted her, and we fought."

Bennett's eyes cast over me. "Except for the mark she left you with her bite, did she leave any other during the fight?"

"None," I said proudly. "It was only for the sake of tradition, without injury."

I glanced down at my shoulder. Her bite mark was closed already, but it was a mating mark and would never fade. "This is better than any of my tattoos," I murmured. "To have been marked by her is a mark I wear with pride."

"Will you get her name tattooed over your heart?" Bennett asked.

"I don't need to, as her name is already tattooed on my heart," I replied.

Gideon rolled his eyes. "Our alpha is lovelorn. Maybe we should take him to see Solstice."

Mason's eyes lit up. "Yes, our alpha needs a new tattoo!" He grabbed his phone, typing into it.

"What are you doing?" I asked.

"We probably shouldn't drive, so hopefully she'll come here!" Mason responded, his eyes twinkling. His phone beeped. "Yes! She's on her way."

I frowned, but Mason's grin only grew wider. "Relax, my brother. You will return to your love's side with another mark to show her."

"One made by another woman," I emphasised.

Bennett shook his head in amusement. "But made in her honour. Will you get her name, or something deeper, like a flower to represent her?"

His question left me stumped. What would I get to represent

my mate? "She's the light of the full moon in the darkest night," I murmured.

"You're too romantic for your own good!" Mason said, and punched me in the shoulder. I punched back, laughing.

"Her beauty knows no bounds!" I declared. "But the way she reached for my cock–"

"He has no shame!" Mason said, cutting me off. "Every word that passes his lips is romantic and sweet, yet dripping with indecency for his flower."

"Not just any flower, a rose," I said. "Beautiful but deadly, with thorns."

They all stared at me in shock. Mason smirked.

"Perhaps he can teach us how to draw in the she-wolves with such pretty words," Bennett added.

Mason wrapped his arm around my throat. I pulled out of his grip, playfully punching him again. His arm came up, blocking my strike before taking a slow swing at me. Laughter burst from me, and Bennett tackled me to the ground. I growled as they all piled on top of me, a sound of play as I struggled to get out from under them.

"Fuck, you made me spill my beer!" Mason climbed to his feet, pulling another bottle from our fridge.

"I hope you're going to clean that up!" I laughed, finally free as everyone else released me.

"And what if I don't?" he asked.

"I'll use my alpha spark and make you stand in the middle of the human town, naked," I said, reaching for a new bottle of my own.

"Promise?" Mason smirked.

"You offer a punishment that he would enjoy!" Bennett said. "The people more shocked would be the humans. Nakedness is not natural to them. He'd have the cops after him again."

We all laughed.

"Oh, but they'd not be able to look away!" Mason said, and pulled off his tee-shirt, revealing his own tattoos. "Can you blame them? They'd want a piece of me." He ran his hand over his own abs. "They'd know hotness when they see it. But I'm too much wolf for them to handle." He grabbed his crotch and grunted. Once again, our laughter echoed around the room.

There was a knock on the front door. Gideon left the room to let Solstice in.

She looked me up and down. "You've come into your alpha power. It sings from you. Did you find your mate?"

"He did," Bennett said. "He hunted her, they fought, but he's yet to fully claim her."

"You want a tattoo to mark the occasion?" she asked, her eyes on me.

Mason pulled my tee-shirt down, showing space over my heart I hadn't yet tattooed. "A moon," he told her. "Maybe with wolf eyes in it. Or a wolf."

"Pity we don't have a photo of her wolf," Gideon said.

Solstice met my eyes. "Your entire energy is focused on her. Damn, I love newly mated wolves, you give off such a power. Mixed with your alpha spark, you're really projecting quite strongly. I can almost see her. Take off your tee-shirt. Lie down."

She laid out her tools as I did as she asked, laying on the kitchen table, staring at the ceiling. Her hand pressed against my chest, warm, sending a slight quiver through me.

"She is beautiful," Solstice noted. "And her energy is wild."

"I'm pretty sure she *is* a Wild," I agreed. "The glint in her eyes suggested as much. Even in human form, her wolf was very close to the surface."

"Why would a Wild be at the Silver Moons–" Mason cut himself off, and the three of them exchanged glances. They'd worked it out, but said nothing. They'd have questions later.

Solstice spent the next hour tattooing me. I stared up at the ceiling, my betas watching as the tattoo took shape. I let the pain wash over me as needle pierced flesh. I'd had so many tattoos I actually enjoyed the pain. Solstice was the only way we could get tattoos. Our healing ability meant the ink would fade into our skin as if it were never there. As a Magic Wielder, she did the same for vampires who sometimes called upon her services.

Finally, she stepped back. I climbed off the table and used the door as a mirror, the darkness behind it enough to give me that reflection. She'd tattooed a moon, with the eyes of a wolf. They were her eyes. Jewel's.

The red would fade quickly, my new tattoo now my favourite. She truly had a place over my heart, and I couldn't wait to show her.

"Thank you, Solstice," I said.

She'd done all of my tattoos. I handed her cash, which she pocketed.

"Your she-wolves will truly be disappointed you're off the market," she commented.

"More for the rest of us!" Mason added. "I'm no stranger to a man or a woman's love, but my heart aches for what my alpha now has."

"Mason has spent years chasing pleasure, and only recently has he questioned where his true love might be," Bennett said with a grin. "Chances are he has already broken their heart."

Mason lost his smirk. It was only for a brief moment, but

I caught it. Bennett had named the very thing that haunted Mason. I wrapped one arm around him.

"He is yet to find his." I attempted to bring back the smile that Mason was so well known for. "He'll meet them in the spring, when packs send their unmated wolves here. With Mason's charm, and as my beta, he'll be irresistible."

Solstice eyed Mason. "It's a pity you only take wolves to be your mates. You're exactly my type. Witty, smug. I'll bet that sharp tongue of yours is good for more than just your words."

Mason's eyes widened, and silver fur rippled across his skin. A low growl rose from him. "Woman, you tease!"

The spark in her eyes was of pure heat and desire. "I am no tease. Care to find out?"

She moved in the direction of his bedroom. The wicked glint in his eyes showed his willingness. "No cubs!" he said as he followed her.

"I'll magically prevent that from happening," she called back. "I know what would happen. I will not do that to any child of a wolf."

Mason's responding growl was raspy, full of lust.

"Do you need company?" Bennett asked me. "An escort to your meeting place?"

"No," I said. "Perhaps now is a good time for you to run the grounds?"

"Make it twice!" Mason shouted from his bedroom. "We're going to be a while!"

"Have fun!" I said with a grin.

I made my way to my bedroom, throwing a blanket into a bag. I paused, looking back at my desk. I opened the drawer, reaching for the ring. I'd found it in town years ago. Marriage wasn't our tradition, and we couldn't maintain jewellery during a shift, but there was meaning there. I'd learned enough about human society to know the romantic aspect of their weddings. I hoped Jewel would like it.

Chapter 11

JEWEL

"An alpha," Eve said. "Not just any alpha, but the one who will lead a pack whose members have been our rivals for generations. They're our enemies, Jewel."

I let her rant and pace. I lay with my head resting on my paws, watching as she moved back and forth before me. I'd never understood why wolves would be enemies with other wolves anyway.

"Oh my Goddess, how will you tell your uncle?" she asked. "Your cousin was enraged that Roman was here in the first place. He's not going to like this at all."

I let out a whine and thumped my tail on the ground.

Eve stopped and faced me. "Jewel, you know what this means? Mating with him means you'll have to lead his pack with him. The Midnight Pack may not let you return home. They may not welcome you at all. Did he tell you any of that? Did he even tell you he was an alpha?"

I shifted so I could talk, pulling the blanket around me. "I've met next-in-line alphas before, and they couldn't wait to boast about it. He didn't. And when I followed him, he didn't care that I was a Silver Moon pack wolf. I only saw tenderness in his eyes. He said we'll talk when I meet him in the valley."

"And you knew beforehand that he was an alpha?" she asked.

I merely smiled. "It's hard to miss the eyes. That's always a dead giveaway. Plus, his voice held sway when he told me to run. His very presence was powerful, yet calming."

Eve sat beside me and gazed into my eyes. "I just worry about you. I'll miss you."

I put my hand on her arm. "I know, and I'll miss you too."

"I don't want you to leave. What if I never see you again?" she asked.

"You will," I promised. "Maybe we can meet in the valley between Silver Moon and Midnight territory."

She took a deep breath and let it out slowly. "I really thought you'd always be here."

My heart broke for her. "This was supposed to be a celebration. Why are you not happy for me?" I asked.

She pulled me into a hug. "I am, Jewel, I really am." Her smile lit up her face. "Especially because you hated the mating hunt. You've always preferred to sit them out. Yet you let him hunt you."

I couldn't hide my joy. "I never thought they'd be so much fun! I actually want him to hunt me again. Oh! Maybe I can hunt him!"

"I told you!" Her smile was genuine, her eyes sparkled, full of joy. "So when you meet him, is he going to hunt for you? Will you mate?" she asked.

"He said we'll hunt together!" I said, excitement filling me.

"He sees you as his equal, not someone to provide for," Eve acknowledged. "I like him already."

"So, will you stop stressing, then?" I asked.

She nodded. "I'm sorry, Jewel, you know I just want to see you happy." She rose to her feet. "Can we run? I can escort you to where you're meeting him. Maybe I can catch a glimpse of him again. That body was definitely one worth marking. Don't you just want to lick him all over?"

Laughter burst from me. "I want to do more than that! He's all mine, and I want to mark him over and over again."

Eve unzipped the jacket she wore. "I'm going to miss our talks," she admitted. "Maybe I'll have to wander down to the boundary line to meet you every now and again."

Eve had been a consistent part of my life ever since I could remember. My earliest memories of her had been before I'd made my first shift. She'd been sitting by the river when I'd wandered off to explore the forest. I was all wolf, and she was the first outside my family I'd seen in human form. She'd shifted, and she'd run with me. I truly would miss her.

"I'll use Roman's phone to message and call you," I promised, wondering if Roman had a phone. I'd chosen the wild existence and hadn't used one in years. Eve had shown me that video calls were now very popular, and that people watched movies on phones.

"Maybe I'll make videos for you?" I hugged her again. "I'll miss you, Evie."

She wiped her eyes. "Oh, sweetie, don't get me all teary-eyed. This isn't a permanent goodbye!" She pulled off her jacket. "Our last run before you become royalty."

We ran for what felt like hours. The Wilds joined us. I'd never seen their human faces, but they were as consistent in my life as Eve. I wondered if Roman had any Wilds in his pack. The idea of running with them filled me with joy.

Finally, I made my way to the place our territories met. I let out a howl as I approached, and he howled back, his voice a delight to every part of me. He was already there! The Wilds left, recognising his howl to be from another pack. I approached him with my head held high, Eve beside me, more reserved than usual. Showing him the respect of the alpha.

As we reached him, she lowered her head. Roman sniffed at her, and she mirrored his actions. Scared that he would see a threat in her presence, I approached him, nuzzling my head under his throat. His head dropped, our foreheads pressed together.

I gave an impatient yip, and Eve turned her head towards me. She bowed to the both of us and bounded away. Finally it was just the two of us. I leapt at Roman, and he playfully tackled me to the ground. I twisted under him, pushing myself off the ground, pinning him under me. Even in wolf form, the amusement and glee flaring in his eyes was unmistakable.

I don't know how long we fought in that playful manner, but

he finally lifted himself from the ground, turning his head, as if looking for something. My tail wagged as I realised what he was doing. It was time to hunt.

Chapter 12

ROMAN

After some playful fighting that left me heated and wanting, we both switched into hunting mode. Her alert movements were instant, her eyes watchful—on me, and our surroundings. I raised my head, breathing in the scents around me. Rabbits and possums were nearby, but I wanted something bigger that we could share. The distinctive musk of deer was faint, but I followed it with a quick pace. Jewel ran at my side, already displaying her desire to be my equal. I had courted wolves before who were all too eager to fall behind me during a hunt. To let me be the alpha. As co-alpha, Jewel would lead equally.

Until that moment, I'd never truly understood what love at first sight would feel like. My parents had explained it, but one could never grasp what it was to experience it until they found the other half of their soul. I'd always worried about putting the weight of my being an alpha on another's shoulders. As I watched Jewel, my chest swelled with utter joy. Warmth flooded every part of me.

We locked onto the deer's trail, and my whole body quivered. I wanted to impress her. But this hunt wasn't about impressing her, it was about proving to each other that we were hunting partners. Equals. That she was my co-alpha.

We caught sight of our prey - a doe - and Jewel lowered her body, moving forward slowly. She lifted her eyes to mine before returning focus to the deer in front of us. I left her side, flanking the deer. As it got near, she leapt towards it, both of us giving chase as the deer bolted. Jewel kept at the animal's heels, while I hoped to get close enough to the beast's throat. Jewel pushed herself through the air, paws outstretched. Her weight on the haunches of the deer pulled it down, and I darted in for its throat.

I let Jewel have the first bite, satisfied at our first hunt. I stood and watched her for a moment, bursting with pride. She stopped mid-chew and tilted her head at me. My mouth dropped into a wide, wolfish grin. Our first hunt together. The first of many. I tore into the carcass, both of us growling as we ate. The two of us devoured our food. I'd gotten my full moon hunt after all.

When we finished, I nuzzled her. She nudged her head under my throat. I pushed my head against her body, turning her around, and walked in the direction I'd just pointed her in. Delighted when she trotted beside me, I picked up speed. We made our way to the cave, where I shifted to human. She shifted too. Her mouth and chin were covered in fresh blood from our kill, and I knew mine would be as well.

Her pale skin almost glowed in the moonlight that shone through a hole in the roof of the cave. With my fingers, I pushed strands of hair from her face. My heart still raced from our hunt, now also fluttering with yearning.

"I'm drunk on love," I whispered. "You're a vision of desire. My Wild Rose."

"I hope you didn't just bring me to this cave to stare at me," she returned, and her lips crashed against mine.

Her fingers flexed through my hair, one hand cupping my cheek. I slid my arms around her lower back. Her body flush against mine, my cock responded to our contact.

"There's a hot spring at the end of this cave," I said. "They're relaxing, and warm. It'll be like having a hot bath. I can wash you," I offered. My fingers brushed up her arm and I caressed her cheek with my thumb. "You're the first woman I've brought here."

Her eyes sparkled, darting over my face. "This place is special to you," she commented.

I nodded. "I found the cave with my betas, and I could think of no place more perfect to bring you." I gave her a small smile. "Wait until you see what's in the cavern."

I took her by the hand, and I led her deep into the back of

the cave. It was pitch black, but my night vision kicked in. We entered a cavern. A blue-green glow reflected from the pool and danced across the walls

Jewel stared at the top of the cave in wonder.

"They're glow worms," I said.

"It's beautiful," she said, squeezing my fingers.

I tucked hair behind her ear. "I thought to be romantic," I replied.

She snapped at my jaw playfully. "You don't need glow worms and a hot spring for that. Your words alone are romantic. You do know how to charm a wolf."

I stroked her cheek with my thumb. "I promised to show you what else I can do with my tongue," I offered. "Then, as you're still trembling from that, I want to bend you over and give you a night you'll never forget. There will be many more to follow."

Her eyes widened, the spark of desire in their depths. "Your words have gone from sweet to spicy!" She pressed her body against mine. "What are you waiting for?"

I stepped into the water, its warmth seeping into me, and held a hand out to Jewel. She took it and I helped her into the hot spring.

"Wow, it is warm," she said.

I led her deeper into the pool, wrapping her in an embrace, the water at our shoulders. As she gazed up at me, her look of hunger sent my heart soaring. I lowered my hand under the water, lifting it to her chin. As I washed the blood from her face, she did the same for me. Her hands slid down to my chest, and our eyes locked. She reached up, grasping my face and pulling it down, her lips parted. Soft, warm and inviting, the kiss sent sparks pulsing, from my mouth to my toes. Heat consumed me, radiating across my chest, and I pressed forward. Her back hit the wall of the pool.

The water was shallower here, to our thighs. I lowered my head to her breast, sucking on her nipple. My hand dropped, my fingers finding her clit, moving in a circular motion, feeling her body instantly react. She let out a little whimper. My top and bottom canines lengthened. A growl rose from me, deep and full of need. I lifted my mouth to her throat. Jewel stilled, and held her head up high as I pressed my teeth into her flesh, not breaking skin. It showed her trust in me. Her hand slid down, pressing my hand firm against where I continued to massage her.

I lifted my mouth from her throat, baring my own. As her mouth closed over my throat, her fingers threaded through my hair. Her lips brushed over my neck and my jaw.

"Is the wall too rough?" I asked.

She shook her head. "I want your tongue where your fingers are," she breathed. "Just like you promised."

Behind her was a ledge wide enough for her to sit on. I grabbed her hips, lifted her onto it, and wrapped my hands around her thighs, pulling them apart. Leaning back, Jewel hooked her ankles behind my head. I gave her my most smug smile and kissed her pussy, licking her gently. I ran my tongue through her centre and sucked on her clit. A startled gasp from her had me lifting my head.

"Don't stop," she murmured. "I wasn't prepared for such…" She trailed off.

"Be a good girl and howl for me," I whispered against her heat. "I want you to howl when you come."

I swirled my tongue up and down and dipped it into her opening, loving the sounds coming from her. She moved herself to grind into my face as I licked her out. With hands gripping her hips, and her slight movements, I sped up my pace. Her breathing intensified.

"Oh, Goddess," she gasped. "Roman, growl for me." Her voice had deepened to a growl of her own.

I let out a deep and rumbling sound that vibrated against her. She whimpered and pushed into my face harder, grinding against my mouth.

"Rougher," she pleaded.

I gripped her tighter, adding more pressure with my tongue. Her breathing quickened again. Claws replaced my fingers, digging into her soft skin. She started to tremble, then her body tensed. She threw her head back, and a howl bounced off the walls of the cave. With her arousal on my face, I smiled up at her. Fine quivers still ran through her body when I pulled her from the ledge, easing myself into her. Jewel's howl cut off as I pulled out and pushed into her again. We built an even rhythm, her body clenching around me.

Black fur rippled across my arms, fading quickly. My wolf was close to the surface, wanting her body with the same intensity I did. I growled again as pleasure started to build up in my gut, surging up to my chest. Our movements grew rough, the two of us giving in to our primal urges. I yearned to bite her, to mark her again. With my hands under her, she wrapped her legs around my waist as I slammed her into the wall.

I kissed her jaw, her throat.

"I need to sink my teeth into something," she grunted. "Roman, I need to mark you again."

I guided her head onto my shoulder, the shiver of fur rippling across her skin. Her canines sank into where she'd already marked me. When she released me, I pulled out and removed her legs from my hips. I turned her around, pressing her shoulders down. With her back horizontal, I re-entered her pussy, my pace fast and savage. Her own movements were just as rough as she rammed herself back to meet my momentum. A mixture of our grunts and moans echoed around the cave.

Our bodies were made for each other and her very presence filled me with warmth. Her soft skin and spring-like scent, mixed with that of her lust, awoke something in me. I was one with my wolf as we claimed her. Heat radiated from my gut and chest, snaking its way around my spine. Each movement of my hips sent waves of euphoria through me. Need, longing and love had me in its grip, and sheer joy that she was mine.

Electricity jolted through me, and I let out a long deep roar as I came. Her own orgasm followed. I pulled out of her, breathing hard, and I held her to my chest.

"Can we lie down?" she asked through pants. "I want to touch you, and feel your arms around me."

I carried her back to where I'd placed the blanket. We lay down together. I brushed my fingers over her cheek. She touched my chest, her hands sliding down, over my ribs and up my back. Then she rested her head on my chest and let out a content sigh.

I smiled. Now that we had completed the mating ritual with the hunt, the marking and sex, the alpha spark that burned inside me blazed. I would soon have to take my place as alpha. This also presented concern for how either of our packs would accept this. But I was happy to lie on the blanket, arms wrapped around her.

"I can't feel my pack any more," she stated. "I can sense you, though."

I couldn't feel mine, either. The absence of my parents' presence was a little strange. It wouldn't be long before our packs sensed our absence. We were two wolves from different packs, and we would have to either choose a pack to join, or form a new one. I already had the alpha spark, and would take the leadership of my pack. I would need to arrange the ceremony in which my parents passed the torch.

I pushed her hair from her face. "Are you okay with that?" I asked. "Leaving your pack to join another is going to be a massive change."

"I'm okay," she confirmed. "My wolf is okay. As long as I have space to run and hunt."

I grinned. "We have plenty of room for that. I have a house, but I've always preferred to be out in the open. There's even a den under the alpha's house. It's where I spent my days as a cub. It's warm and dry, if we need it for shelter."

Her arms around me tightened. "Then I'm happy," she agreed. "Roman, my alpha, once you've presented me to your pack, we'll never be apart."

My joy dimmed slightly. Now I just had to figure out how to tell my pack that we had a Silver Moon for my co-alpha.

Chapter 13

ROMAN

With Jewel in my arms, our warm bodies pressed against each other, I let myself doze off.

When I opened my eyes, half the blanket had been pulled over us. Jewel snuggled into my body, my arms around her.

"We don't have much time before we have to go back," I murmured.

"How are we going to do this?" she asked. "Our families hate each other; our packs will never come together for this."

I hummed in agreement. "I don't know," I admitted. "I really imagined the day I could present my mate to my pack, and take my role as alpha. I have my betas, ready to step into their roles. It doesn't matter *to me* what pack you're from. It won't matter to my betas, either."

"What if they attack me?" she asked.

"Then I will defend you," I promised.

"This is our final moment before all that, then," she whispered. "Here. Now. I never want this to end."

"Me neither," I agreed, and lowered my head to kiss her. "Your breath fills me with life. Your lips awaken a deep need."

She grinned. "There you are, trying to charm me with your words again."

I brushed my fingers down her arm, a soft caress. "I like what my words do to you," I admitted. "I love the way your heart flutters and your eyes light up." I brushed her arm again. "Same as when I do *this;* I can feel the shiver run through you." I brought our lips together in a soft kiss. "But this sends heat through us both."

She let out a deep sigh. "Your very presence has my wolf howling with happiness. I see us hunting together like we did before, a perfect match."

I dropped my kisses to her throat, nipping gently. She quivered against me, whimpering. I touched the back of her neck, running my fingers over the mark I'd left there. My grip tightened, and I growled in her ear. Another shiver tore through her, and she groaned.

A perfect match. It would just be the two of us. I closed my eyes, content.

"You fell asleep again," she whispered. "Did you eat too much?"

I grinned. "I certainly ate a fair amount."

Laughter burst from her.

"The humans have a term: 'food coma'," I said. "We ate a whole deer between us. I am a little drowsy."

She moved her hands: one lay on my hip, the other against my chest, where her head also rested. Her warm breath brushed my skin.

"I can't remember the last time I slept in human form," Jewel admitted. "It feels strange. I do like waking up in your arms though. I felt safe, protected. My wolf didn't feel the need to shift at all."

I tightened my arms around her. "I'll protect you as long as you need me to," I promised.

She stretched. "I wish I could stay here with you. What do we do next?"

I kissed her forehead. "Let me talk to my alphas," I said. "I need to tell them that I have found a mate. I need them to recognise my power as a rising alpha."

"I've never seen an alpha step into the role," she noted.

I hadn't either, but I'd been told what to expect. "When I present you to the alphas, and the pack, they must kneel to both of us. My betas will kneel first. Any of the pack who remain standing are rejecting either me or my mate. My parents will be the last ones to kneel. In doing so, they're recognising me as the new alpha of the pack. I'll feel the transfer of power, and so will you."

"Alpha. I never imagined this was my fate," she acknowledged.

I kissed her again. "This is a lot to put on anyone. Do you regret–"

"No!" she insisted. "How can I regret finding a piece of my heart? My companion meant for me? It would destroy my very soul to deny you." Her eyes gazed longingly into mine. "I loved you from that first kiss, and I knew I'd found my mate. The only one worthy to chase and mark me."

I laughed. "You made me work for that!"

She pinned me beneath her. "You didn't think I'd make it easy for you, did you?"

Her fingers brushed my shoulder, where she'd marked me. When she lowered her lips, kissing the mark, I groaned. Her kisses moved up to my throat, where she nipped me as I'd done to her. Love bites. I reached up, my hand over my mark on the back of her neck.

"I should go," I murmured.

"You should," she agreed, smirking at me.

"Are you going to make me work for that too?" I asked.

She leaned down and kissed me. "Every day," she said against my mouth. "I'm going to make you work *every day*."

I grabbed her hips and flipped us over. "Then I will devote myself to being worthy of you. My heart, my alpha, my Wild Rose. You will be a queen in my home. *Our* home." I lifted myself from her, and grabbed the metal circle I'd stored under the blanket.

She sat up, watching me, and I took a knee.

"The humans have different rituals to us, where they seal their love with a ring," I said. "They have a ceremony, where they talk about how they love each other. They exchange rings, and they are united in what they call 'marriage'." I held the ring out to her. "Even though you can't wear it forever, like the humans do, would you accept this ring and let me put it on your finger?"

She held her hand out in silence. I slipped it over her finger, hoping I was doing it the right way.

"Then they end their ritual with a kiss," I said and kissed her hard.

She smiled. "I've seen this in movies. They're not usually naked, though. If there is a woman, she wears a white dress, and if there is a man, he wears a very uncomfortable-looking suit. There are flowers, and their whole pack is there."

"They don't call them packs," I kissed her again. "But do you want a white dress? With the flowers?"

She shook her head. "I like it better with us naked. Does this make us married?" she asked. "Like the humans?"

I laughed. "I gave you my ring, and we kissed. That's good enough for me."

"We'd never be able to live like them, in their world," she said. "Our eyes would scare them."

I laughed. "I sometimes have to go into town and we have to cover our eyes. I have to wear clothes. They don't like nakedness outside of the bedroom."

"I haven't worn human clothes in years," she told me. "When I shift, I mostly just wrap myself in a blanket if it's cold. I don't actually own any clothes, I've never been into the town. My friend Eve has a house, with a mate. Her cubs live in the den underneath the house. She's let me watch her TV."

I squeezed her hand gently. "I'll never make you wear clothes if you don't want to," I promised. "If you ever want to go with me into the town, though, we can ride my motorbike." I thought of her on my bike, the heat of her body pressed against my back.

She gave me a wide smile. "Do you have a spare helmet and leather jacket for me, then?"

Oh fuck. Her in a leather jacket and helmet was definitely something I wanted to see. "I'll ride into town today to pick one up for you," I promised. "Do you prefer dresses, or jeans and tee-shirts?"

"Can we just lie here a little longer?" she asked. "I like basking in your company. I like listening to your voice, and breathing in your scent."

I lay down beside her again. She held her hand up, examining the ring. "I really wish I could wear this forever. When I return home, I'll leave this here so I can come back for it. She touched my chest, her fingers a soft caress. "You have so many tattoos." Her hand paused over the moon. "This one is new."

"I needed it to represent you," I said. "Those are your eyes in the moon."

She studied the tattoo. "How did the person who did this know my eyes?"

I caressed her face. "Solstice is a Magic Wielder. She can see things that humans can't. By placing her hand over my heart, she saw you. She knew that I'd found my mate."

"What are the others for?" she asked.

I pointed to the one across my chest. "This one's me. The forest and river are where I spend much of my time."

"I recognise your wolf. Maybe Solstice can add me to that one," she said.

I kissed her fingers, then indicated the crescent moon on my shoulder. It was the same image we used for our farm logo. "This is the symbol of my pack. We use a similar symbol that the humans see as our farm logo. Only it has an M in it. I got the

Greek letter alpha." I pointed to each tattoo as I talked about them. "The motorbike is because it's the only way that I can get remotely close to that rush of speed. The dagger just seemed cool. That was my first tattoo. Solstice suggested the vine of thorns around it. The heart with the arrow through it was after I read a book about Cupid, and how he shoots arrows through hearts to make them fall in love. My beta Mason suggested that. He said I'm romantic and that Cupid would find me an easy mark."

Jewel laughed. "Well, you were a charmer with your words when we first met. It was difficult to remain guarded, from the moment your mouth opened."

I grinned. "I accidentally tapped into my alpha spark when I was trying to hold back the shift. So you would have felt the power of my alpha voice."

"I felt it," she confirmed.

I continued showing her my tattoos, pointing to my abs. "The skull is to represent our own mortality. We do live longer than humans, but we're still mortal like they are. Only vampires have that immortality." I lifted my inner wrist where a V had been tattooed with yellow eyes and canines.

"This one represents me and my betas. An alpha relies on his or her betas. For advice, for safety. They take an oath to protect their alpha. They're like brothers."

Jewel traced circles over my chest. "My cousin says the same about his betas."

Her cousin. Tyler. That was going to be a difficult challenge, facing him. It was on me to inform the alphas of her pack that I'd taken Jewel for my mate. The moment I entered his territory, Tyler would see it as a threat.

Chapter 14

JEWEL

I'd mated a few times, as a wolf, but I had never experienced sex in human form. I would never have imagined the pleasure would be so intense. Roman pulled me from the floor.

"Can't we stay here a little longer?" I asked.

I didn't want to go back to my pack. I didn't want to have to tell them what had happened. Parker had spent years trying to lay claim to me. Would this be enough for him to back off?

Roman pressed his lips to my forehead. "Meet me back here tomorrow at midnight. We'll hunt again if you want, or we can just run. Then I'll grant you access to my territory, and we can meet my pack."

That meant his current alphas too. His parents. Worry filled me again about the rivalry between our packs. I wanted my family to be there to see me join Roman's pack. To witness him becoming an alpha, and myself.

I'd never been ambitious. Alpha was my cousin's fate, and all I'd ever wanted was the freedom to simply exist as a wolf.

"Okay," I agreed.

Roman's hand tightened on mine before letting go. I removed the ring he'd given me. A secret human wedding between the two of us was as romantic as the glow worms in the cavern beside the pool. I didn't have human needs, but had to admit I liked this. I placed the ring where I would find it again, under the blanket.

We shifted, then left the cave. He whined, and pressed his head into my neck, a gentle nudge. He wanted to stay as much as I did. I licked at his muzzle and turned, running before I decided to follow him into his territory. I didn't look back.

I knew Eve would be waiting for me. Sure enough, as I got to my usual place at the river, I caught sight of the familiar wolf form in the early dawn. She lifted her head when I arrived. Her expression was almost quizzical. I let my mouth fall into a smile, and she mirrored me. I shifted and grabbed the blanket still there from Eve's last visit, wrapping it around me. The blanket was light, waterproof but warm. Eve took her human form and sat beside me, pulling the other half of the blanket over her own shoulders.

"Tell me everything?" she asked.

"We hunted. I have to admit we were in tune with each other. We are great hunting partners. He didn't lead the hunt. He even let me take the first bite of our kill," I blurted, and filled her in on every detail.

"He ate you out?" Eve's eyes practically glimmered. "How was he? Satisfying, I hope!"

I nodded. "There's so much I didn't expect. The size of him, for starters." A wide grin spread across my face.

Laughter burst from her. "I could have guessed he was a big boy. Probably a gift of his alpha gene." Her expression changed, becoming serious. "Do you want me with you when you tell your family?"

I hadn't been inside my parents' house in years. I stood. "No, this is for me to do alone. Thank you for the offer, though."

Eve reached out to me. "You're leaving behind everything that you know," she said. "Are you sure you're okay with this?"

I gave her a smile. "The thing with being a Wild, all we need is space to run."

"But this is your home, Jewel," she said.

"I'm not like you. I didn't make a home, nor a den like you. I don't have a bed," I reminded her. "Moving to a new territory will be a lot to adjust to, but the Wild in me will adjust quickly enough. This was always my fate, anyway. If our mate isn't in our pack, we go to their territory. Your home was always supposed to be here. Mine's with Roman now. *If* his pack will accept me."

She gave me a sad smile. "I'm sure they will," she said with a soothing tone. "Can a pack deny an alpha's mate?"

I recalled what Roman had told me. "If they do, they're denying his right to ascend to alpha," I replied.

I hugged her, and I shifted again. I would have to tell not only my parents, but also my uncle. Probably my cousin too. But it was the other Wilds I needed to see before I left. I let out a howl, and their replies echoed around me. Despite our pack already having alphas, whom even Wilds respected, there was a wolf who seemed to lead the Wilds. I didn't know her name, nor if she even had one. She was a large animal, black and grey. I'd discussed with Eve many times who she was. Eve suspected she was a relative. Only the blood of an alpha could present that power. My father was the only sibling to our alpha that I knew of, but she did seem familiar. I approached her, my head and eyes low. She circled me, sniffing me, and she whined. I figured she could tell I'd mated. Other wolves approached, sniffing me. Five Wilds surrounded me, and they let out a haunting howl. We were saying goodbye. If I'd been in human form, I may have shed tears. This was my family; this was the pack I'd miss, as well as Tyler and Eve.

The large wolf ran, and I couldn't resist one last run with them. I bounded after the wolves, noticing a new one I hadn't noticed before. He turned his head, his wolf-like smile unsettling for some reason. *Parker.* I kept my distance, but he kept wandering closer. The very action took away the enjoyment of the run. I broke away from the pack and bolted. I could hear him behind me. He wasn't moving as fast, though. I found the hole I often slept in and hid as he ran past.

It didn't take him long to work out he'd lost me before his human voice echoed through the forest, calling my name. I avoided him, and finally made my way towards where my parents lived. The house was as I remembered it. There were familiar scents. Parker, my parents, my aunt and uncle, and even Tyler.

I raised my paw, scratching at the door. Were they inside, or somewhere else? But the door swung open, and my mother smiled down at me. Warmth from the house and comforting scents surrounded me.

"Jewel," she said, her eyes shining. She crouched down to meet my eyes. "Welcome home." She held her arms open, and I rushed in to let her embrace me.

Her gentle voice and fruity scent filled me with memories from my cubhood.

"Will you come inside?" she asked, as she rose to her feet, holding out a blanket.

My ears pinned back as I stared inside.

"Maybe the den?" she added.

I led the way to the den. I felt safer in the den that had been dug in below the house. There were only dirt walls, with no door to make me feel trapped.

I shifted, taking the blanket from her and wrapping it around myself.

"Wow, you look so different," Mum observed, handing me the blanket. "You're not a teenager any more, but a young woman. Your hair is longer. Are you hungry?"

I smiled. "I'm okay. Where's Dad?"

"He's with his brother. Some Midnight wolves were here last night, and the alphas see it as a challenge," she explained.

"How is that any different to Tyler leading wolves onto their territory?" I asked.

"You heard about that?" She stared at me in silence for a long minute. "You're right. Your hot-headed cousin shouldn't have done that. They didn't invade, the way those young wolves did last night, though."

My chest tightened. She *really* wasn't going to like what I'd come here to tell her.

Mum unexpectedly stepped up to me, sniffing. Her eyes widened. "You've mated!"

Hands shaking, I lifted the hair from the back of my neck, and showed her Roman's mark.

Her fingers brushed over where Roman had bitten me. "You've been marked! Oh Jewel, congratulations. When did this happen?" Tears welled up in her eyes, and she pulled me into another hug.

"Last night, during the pairing ceremony," I said.

"Oh, I didn't realise you were here for that." Her voice burst with joy.

"I made the expected appearance, then tried to make my escape and hide like I usually do," I confessed. "But he followed me."

Laughter shone in her eyes. "Of course you did. So who is he? Will you have to leave for a new territory? Oh, is it that Parker kid? He's always been convinced you were his. Was he right?"

I opened my mouth but hesitated. She looked so overjoyed at the idea that Parker was the one. I sighed.

"I think you should sit down, Mum. I'm not sure you're going to like what I'm about to tell you."

Chapter 15

ROMAN

I reached my house as the sky started to lighten. Gideon and Bennett greeted me at the door, eyes lingering on me, watchful. Gideon sniffed at me, not attempting to hold back his smirk.

I shifted, accepting the clothes they offered me. I pulled on the grey track pants, black tee-shirt, and my Swanndri. Deep breathing sounded from Mason's room. Only one heartbeat, though.

"Where's Mason?" I asked.

"He's at the gates. Wolves howled for support, so he led others to investigate," Bennett explained.

"Support for what?" I asked. "Should we be concerned?"

Gideon shook his head. "Nah, newly shifted cubs possibly just testing their voice. Probably got startled by a possum or something. Mason will let us know if he needs backup."

If that were so, Mason should have returned by now. Something didn't feel right. "Let's go check it out, just in case," I said.

Bennett didn't hesitate. "Wheels or on paws?"

"This is pack business, so I should probably not show up violating the alpha's orders," I suggested, and pulled on my boots.

We piled into the ute, and Bennett broke human speeding laws to get to our gates. There, I found Tyler and his betas in a confrontation with Mason and some younger wolves. Silver fur rippled over Mason's arms and face, fury darkening his eyes.

"Your alpha is here," Tyler said to Mason. "Perhaps he's not the gutless cub I thought he was."

I didn't wait for Bennett to bring the ute to a stop before I was running towards Tyler and Mason.

"Tyler, what's this about?" I asked, aware of Tyler's betas flanking him. "Do you not grow tired of the violence between our packs? Do any of us actually remember the cause for the hate? It was long before we were born. Today, I warmly call you brother, so we can put aside this never-ending hate." I held my hand out, as if to shake his.

"You arrogant fuck!" Tyler screamed, knocking my hand aside. "You were in our territory last night! I heard you howl. Someone marked territory. Shift, so we can fight."

I breathed in and out, trying to stay calm, as my parents had taught me. I was about to become alpha, I had to show my pack I could handle conflict with Silver Moons. Especially Tyler. The idea of creating a truce with him so Jewel didn't have to fear joining my pack helped keep me level-headed.

"That was me," Mason said laughing. "My mistake, I thought you'd see the humour in it."

"Humour?" Fur rippled across Tyler's skin, his canines lengthening. "You were in my territory." His nostrils flared as he gave Mason a cold stare. He turned his attention to me. "Shift. Fight me. You come to my territory to challenge me? Well, challenge accepted. Here I am!"

With no desire to fight Jewel's cousin, I needed a way to de-escalate the tensions between our packs. If not for the sake of peace, for Jewel.

"I won't fight you," I declared. "Why don't we calm ourselves? We have reason to be brothers. We will soon both be alphas. I call a truce." I spoke as calmly as I could, clutching at hope that he'd see reason.

"A truce?" Tyler growled. "There is no truce! You are no brother to me. Stop stalling, fight me now," he demanded.

"No. Go home, Tyler." I turned my back on Tyler, dismissing him.

"I'll fight you," Mason declared.

Tyler scoffed. "Why would I fight you? A beta? Yeah, right."

I needed to say something. Jewel should be the one to tell him, but with his challenge, and insults to my beta, I needed to put an end to his provocation. I turned towards Tyler again, but before I could say anything, he charged at me, knocking me to the ground. Pinning me with his knees, he swung at my face. Again and again. Claws sprang free, and he slashed at my cheek.

Mason's whole weight hit Tyler, taking him off me. They faced each other, fur rippling, growls rumbling from them.

Gideon helped me up, eyes narrowed. "Roman, you have to do something. This is a declaration of war," he stated. "He doesn't want peace. We have to meet this intrusion head-on."

Midnight Wolves advanced, bodies low to the ground. Growls rose from them, but they could not attack without command. I wasn't alpha yet, so I could not give that order. Frustration choked me as I took in the scene before me.

"Mason!" I called out. "Stop. Now is the time for a truce between our packs."

Tyler pushed Mason out of his way and advanced on me. "Why? You offend me with your presence on *my* territory. Would you let such an insult go?"

I bared my canines at him. "You dare ask me that, a day after you attacked Midnight wolves on our territory!?"

"Protect the alpha!" Mason shouted as Tyler barrelled towards me again, and my pack moved forward, ready to protect me.

Tyler pulled a knife from his belt. I growled. *Silver.* Before I could shift and attack, Mason leapt in between us.

The two wrestled, and Gideon pulled me back. "Let us protect you," he said. "You need to call for your parents. *Now,* Roman!"

Snarls filled the air, then a yelp. Dizzy with panic, I pushed past Gideon. Tyler and Mason fell to the ground, neither of them moving. Mason pinned Tyler beneath him. Bennett and Gideon were at my side, lifting Mason from Tyler. Deep red slashes in Mason's chest sent ice plunging through my chest. But it was the blade sticking from his side that really chilled me to my very soul. Tyler rose to his feet, staring at Mason in horror. I shoved him away.

"Mason?" My voice broke.

Mason opened his eyes, groaning in pain. He pulled the knife out before we could stop him. I pressed my hand to the wound, warm blood gushing through my fingers.

"Bro?" Bennett asked.

"Get Solstice." I grunted out the order, struggling to breathe.

"She's still at our house," Gideon murmured from beside me. "I'll go." He met my eyes. "Call your parents. This has already gone too far."

Gideon shifted and ran, his speed spurred by the same panic crushing against my chest.

"Mason, I didn't want this to escalate." I said, pressing my hand against his wound.

"I'm fine," he gasped, another groan falling from his mouth. "He barely got me. Help me up."

Bennett and I helped him to his feet. Mason pushed away from us, walking back to our territory. "Solstice said blood would be spilled, I didn't know she meant mine."

Solstice had predicted pain and tragedy. *Oh, Goddess, no.*

I ran to Mason. "Please, you know I never wanted this. Jewel is his cousin; I didn't want to fight with the family of my mate."

"My cousin?" Tyler clenched his fists, but didn't move closer. "What did you do to my cousin? Stay away from her!"

Wolves moved between us, growling at Tyler. He backed up.

"I never thought this feud with the Silver Moons would be

my end," Mason said with a weak voice.

His words left me winded as Mason stumbled towards the ute.

"Roman, don't let me die alone," Mason pleaded. "Brother..." He coughed up blood.

"You're not alone," I comforted him. "We're here. Gideon's bringing Solstice."

"I fear when she arrives, I'll already be bound for my grave," he said.

He shifted into a wolf and flopped to his side. Bennett joined me as we knelt over Mason. He whimpered and let out a mournful howl. Wolves around us added their voices to his. Other voices across the land added to the sound. A hot tear ran down my cheek, pain tearing through my heart. Mason wasn't just my beta; he was my closest friend. We'd declared ourselves brothers. I lifted my head to the sky and let out a howl, putting all my pain into it.

Mason could no longer hold his head up, his breaths coming in quick pants.

"Mason, I'm sorry," I whispered.

He whimpered again, and his eyes closed. Tears slid down my cheeks as I ran my hands over his fur. His chest stilled. The beating of his heart became a roaring silence.

Wracked by guilt, I rose to my feet, backing away. Bennett looked up at me, his expression grief-stricken. "He's dead, Roman." His voice broke.

Chapter 16

ROMAN

Tyler and his betas were surrounded by my pack. More wolves advanced, summoned by Mason's dying howl. They provided a barrier. Either to protect me, or to protect Tyler from me, or both. I fought against the rising urge to lunge at him, to tear out his throat. My wolf fought me, struggling to break free, my canines sharpening in my mouth in anticipation of the kill.

I ran shaking hands through Mason's fur.

"Where is she?" I whispered, my voice cracking.

As if to answer my question, Solstice arrived. She knelt over Mason, and the wolves around me whimpered. My grief threatened to drown me. Bennett's words played over and over, and I didn't want to believe Mason was gone. He couldn't be.

"Can you help him?" I pleaded. "Solstice, you're a healer, please help him!"

Blood matted Mason's fur, and I waited for his chest to rise, hoping Bennett was wrong.

"He's already dead," Solstice replied, her tone gentle, pained. "I'm sorry, Roman, I can't bring back the dead." A single tear welled in her eye, and she wiped it away.

I swallowed past a lump in my throat. Memories of our friendship overwhelmed me. Mason being there the first time I shifted. His oath to protect me, to be my beta. The five of us, hunting together. Mason showing me his flirting techniques. Buying our motorbikes. He couldn't be dead.

"But vampires can!" I said. "Someone get Spencer. He can help him!" No one moved, and I glared at Gideon and Bennett, who were on their knees on the other side of Mason. "Now! Get him *now!*" My voice came out raw.

Solstice put a hand to my arm. "Roman, for vampire blood to bring someone back, there would need to be an exchange of blood *before* death. It won't bring him back. Besides, would you really do that to your brother? Would he want that? To be a wolf *and* a vampire?"

I had no idea what vampire blood would do to our kind, if the wolf would even survive through the change, or if he'd become some kind of blend of vampire and wolf. She was right: either way, Mason wouldn't want that.

"If anything would have had the power to help him, it would have been *your* bite," she whispered. "And in doing so, you would have created a new pack."

The alpha bite. I'd heard the stories about how the alpha bite could bring a wolf from the *brink* of death. It was too late for that now. I'd failed Mason, but there I was, seeking ways to bring him back.

I let out another howl; the sound turning into a scream. A couple of wolves whined, nudging at me. Tyler's voice pierced the fog of my anger and grief as he growled and threatened my pack. Had he been doing that the whole time? I raised my eyes to Tyler and his betas.

"You!" I growled. "I'll kill you!"

I'd never thought myself capable of killing someone, but in that moment, white-hot rage pushed out all calm and reason. I advanced on him, ignoring Bennett and Gideon's pleas. I grabbed the knife that Mason had pulled out of himself. I threw it, and the blade embedded in Tyler's shoulder. Not a mortal wound, but it would still be painful, and it would take longer to heal. He wouldn't be alive long enough for that, anyway.

Bennett grabbed my arm. "Roman, don't do anything stupid. We must mourn Mason. The alphas will deal with him."

I dug deep into my alpha spark. "Back off," I growled. "The killer of Mason must die."

Bennett's hand dropped. I shifted, shredding my clothes. Then, without hesitation, I darted towards Tyler. A small voice of reason at the back of my mind told me I should do as my parents had trained me. To show mercy. Even rival packs never actually killed one another. In the years we had lived here, no wolf had been killed by either pack. Mason was the first to die at the hands of another wolf.

I gave in to my devastation, letting anger wash over me. As if realising he was in trouble, Tyler shifted and fled from me. *Coward!* I gave chase, ready to kill, snarling as I pursued him.

"Roman! No!" Gideon shouted behind me, but I didn't turn around, didn't stop. I had Tyler in my sights. I would tear him apart.

Desperation and survival instincts would have fuelled Tyler. Grief and blind rage fuelled me. I dug in deep, put all my strength and speed into catching up with him. Slowly, I started to gain on Tyler. I pushed harder.

I rammed into him hard. His growls were the same as mine. We bared our canines at each other. I lunged for him, and he darted out of my way. I twisted my body to face him in time for his attack. I leapt at him. Snarling in warning, I clamped my teeth on his shoulder. The same one I'd already wounded. He yelped and wrenched out of my grip.

We snapped our jaws, each aiming for the other's throat. I lunged again, pinning him beneath me. I bared my canines. His hind legs connected with my stomach, the impact enough to make me lose my footing. Before I could move, he pinned me, his bared canines inches from my throat.

The sound of a vehicle and human voices calling our names drew Tyler's attention. He lifted his head in the direction of the sound. With his throat exposed, I lunged, sinking my teeth into the vulnerable spot. Tyler yelped and struggled to free himself.

"Roman, stop!" Bennett pleaded.

I shook my head, growling and biting deeper. Flesh tore and

blood gushed over my muzzle from the wound I'd made. I opened his throat, and he collapsed on top of me. I struggled out from under him, glaring down at the fallen wolf. He whimpered, blood pouring from him, eyes gazing up at me. I stood over him triumphantly.

"Roman, what have you done?" Gideon asked in a quiet voice.

I lifted my head and growled. Bennett and Gideon dropped to their knees, bowing their heads in submission.

"You killed another wolf, Roman." Bennett's voice shook.

"There's no coming back from that," Gideon added, his voice barely audible.

I glanced down, finding that life had faded from Tyler's eyes. His stillness pulled me out of my fury. Unable to take my eyes from him, I whimpered. I'd killed. While lupine in nature, we were not cold-blooded killers.

Bennett's hand ran through my coat. "I know. Everything will be alright. Your parents are already on their way, I heard them howl just after you left."

I hadn't heard anything. I'd been so focused on killing. I stared at Tyler's body, shock flooding me.

Footsteps approached. "Our pack is coming," one of Tyler's betas said. "We need to take his body." He spoke to Bennett, avoiding looking at me. "Your alpha probably shouldn't be here with Tyler's blood still dripping from his muzzle. They'll want blood for blood."

Bennett growled. "This *was* blood for blood," he yelled, pointing down at Tyler's body. "Tyler killed *first*." He glanced down at me. "He's right though, Roman. You need to run. They won't enter our territory, but they will demand your death."

I tore my gaze from Tyler and ran.

Chapter 17

JEWEL

"The next alpha?" Mum repeated, rubbing her eyebrow. "Of the Midnight Pack? Roman Morrison. Are you sure?"

I laughed. "I'm pretty sure."

I told her of how I'd met Roman, and the conversation that

followed before he gave chase.

"I always thought you hated the idea of being hunted," she said.

I sipped at the hot drink she'd brought down to me. The aroma and taste of cinnamon combined with coffee filled me with joy.

"I did," I admitted with a slight laugh. "That was before I met Roman. It all changed when he spoke to me and I looked into his eyes. I realised then how strong the mating bond is. I know they're our rival pack, but we can't ignore that bond."

She stood and paced for a few minutes. I watched her in silence. I'd been expecting this. "When will you tell the alphas?" she asked.

I shrugged. "After I've spoken to you, I guess."

"But you'll have to join his pack," she added. "Jewel, I'm not sure your uncle, or even your father, will agree to that."

I rose to my feet. "As powerful as an alpha is, they don't have the ability to go against fate," I affirmed.

She shook her head. "I know your cousin isn't going to be too fond of this."

I could tell she was trying to accept what I'd told her, but she was also trying to find obstacles for me joining my mate.

Noise started up amongst the pack. Something cold crawled through me, with a weight pressing against my chest. All thoughts turned to Roman. I'd heard stories of the bond alphas formed with their mates, fuelled by the alpha spark. Panic overcame me, and I shifted before I could stop myself

"Jewel, it's okay," Mum reassured me.

Dad marched in. His eyes rested on me, his smile full of warmth for a brief moment. "Our alphas demand our support," he declared. "A wolf of the Midnight Pack has been killed.

Tyler killed him. It's likely they'll want a life for a life."

"Where?" Mum asked.

"At their territory. Jackson had his phone and sent a text message." Dad glanced at me. "Jewel, are you with us?"

Mum grabbed his arm. "She can't be." she said. "She's been marked by the up-and-coming alpha of the Midnight Pack. Roman. They've mated."

He stared down at me, all traces of warmth fading. A cold fury darkened his gaze. "You mated with our enemy?" he demanded.

I was glad to be in wolf form so I couldn't answer. I whined instead.

"We don't have time for this," he grunted. "We have to go, Arabella. Now!"

He left. Mum glanced at me once and ran outside. Wolves howled and voices echoed. The alphas howled; then there was silence. Everyone had left. The entire pack. Whatever had happened, I hoped Roman was okay. Someone had been killed. I could no longer go with my pack, but maybe I should go for Roman's sake. *What if he's the one who was killed?* My heart started to race at the very idea. *No!* But he would be in pain if a member of his pack had been killed.

Devastated that Tyler had killed someone, I hoped to see him before he faced his punishment. Would the Midnight pack kill him? I left the den and started to head in the direction of Roman's territory, but I hesitated. I would not be a welcome sight to his pack. Instead, I made my way to the river, taking comfort in the presence of the Wilds. As they ran, they communicated to each other. Wolves who found a home in the wilderness, deciding to stay there, not adhering to the rules of the pack. But nothing could change that this was my first home. A familiar warmth washed over me, and I lay down and closed my eyes.

"Stay back. If she senses anger, she'll feel threatened." A voice pulled me out of my sleep. I lifted my head. Mum walked towards me, wrapped in a blanket.

Dad stood back, watching. They'd returned. How long had I been asleep? I caught the scent of blood.

"Jewel, I need you to stay calm," Mum said. "I have some bad news for you."

Oh, Goddess, something had happened to Roman! And I'd slept through it instead of being there for him. I lowered my head to brace myself for whatever she was about to tell me.

Regret filtered through Mum's eyes. "Jewel, Tyler's been killed. Roman killed him."

Her words were a punch to my chest. *What? No!* I whimpered.

Tyler had taken me on my first hunt. He'd sat with me the day I left the den, telling me about the Wilds. That sometimes when wolves joined them, they didn't come back. He had been as big a part of my life as Eve had. How could he be dead?

"Your uncle calls for Roman's life," Mum continued.

I bolted past Mum, and just managed to get by my father. I didn't want to hear their words, nor what my uncle wanted for the loss of his son. I should have run towards the cave, and hidden until Roman showed up. Afraid he wouldn't, I ran to the bridge where I'd first met him. I lay down, resting my head on my paws, staring at the river. The blanket I'd dropped still lay on the bridge. I shifted, and pulled it around me. My face stung from the icy wind, so I pulled the blanket up to shield my face.

Footsteps behind me alerted me of Eve's approach. She sat

down next to me.

"Is it true?" I asked, not looking at her.

She wrapped her arms around me, an awkward hug. "It is. I saw his body. Roman's cousin explained that he had tried to stop him. But once Tyler killed Mason, Roman couldn't be reasoned with. An alpha lost his beta. He was grieving and gave in to a feral need in his grief."

"Now what am I supposed to do?" I muttered to the water. "Turn on my mate? Ask him how he could take the life of another wolf?"

"Your uncle and aunt have declared that the only way they will allow him to live, is if he gives up his title and his territory," Eve confided. "The Midnight alphas have agreed to banish their son."

I gasped. A wolf being banished from their home was a big deal. Why had my parents not said anything? I absorbed her words silently. They wanted to kill him or banish him. What would that mean for me?

"What about me?" I asked. "Will I be banished with him? I told my parents that he'd marked me and that we'd mated. I have to go and see him."

Eve lowered her voice. "You can't. They'll follow you. Tyler's betas. The entire pack has heard that you let a Midnight wolf mark you. They're angry, and they will know wherever you go, it will be to him." She hesitated. "They won't follow me, though. I can get a message to him."

Hope blossomed in my chest, quickly turning sour. Eve wouldn't betray me, would she? I studied her friendly smile.

"Please don't hurt him," I said.

Her smile faded, turning to shock. "Jewel, no. I would never–"

"I know." I sighed in relief. "I'm just scared. Go see if he's in the place you escorted me to. In the valley is a cave. He won't believe you're there for me unless you say something he'll know has come from me." I had an idea. "There's a ring. When you walk in, it's under the blanket. If you find it, give it to him. He'll know that I told you about it."

"A ring?" she asked.

"A small gold circle," I said. "It goes on your finger. He told me about how humans seal their love, so we did that."

"You married him?" she asked.

I nodded.

She met my eyes. "What do you want me to tell him when I'm there?"

"Wait for me," I said, tears falling down my cheeks. "I'll be here when we agreed. If I'm not, you have to run." If my pack was after me, how would I see him without someone following?

Eve wiped a hot tear from my cheek. "You will see your alpha again. Where will you go until then?"

"I'll run with the Wilds," I said. "That way, anyone following me will give up. They'll think I've returned to what I'm most comfortable with."

She stood up. "Be careful, Jewel. You're practically a rogue wolf right now. Mated to a wolf who killed our next alpha."

She ran off. I dropped the blanket. I would see Roman soon. Until then, I had to hide. The Wilds would help me.

Chapter 18

ROMAN

I ran through the river to cover my trail. The icy water hurt. I needed to get into the cave. The hot spring would warm me, and I could hide. Hopefully Jewel would still meet me. I shifted, stumbling through the water. My own heart was heavy; I feared what would happen when Jewel found out what

I'd done. I'd taken a life and feared my time was short.

I made it to the cave, and sank into the hot spring. As I let myself warm, I struggled to breathe. I'd killed someone. The knowledge threatened to drown me.

Goddess, please forgive me. It was forbidden to kill another wolf. I wondered if the stories were true that one who did kill, would be cursed. The humans' stories about werewolves ran through my mind. Giant creatures covered in fur, on their hind legs, massive wolf heads, and larger than normal canines. *Please don't curse me. I took the blood of the wolf who killed my beta. Blood for blood.*

I leaned my head back and closed my eyes. The hot spring warmed my body, but a chill had pierced my heart. Would Jewel still want me after I'd killed her cousin? What would come of our fate if I'd ruined everything?

Footsteps echoed through the cave. Someone had found me. I held back a growl and left the water, shifting into my wolf form. It was probably Bennett or Gideon, but it couldn't hurt to be cautious. I crept towards the main cave.

A woman lifted the blanket from the ground. I could tell by her scent she was a wolf. I'd seen her before, talking to Jewel. She seemed to be looking for something. Then she reached down, lifting up the gold ring I'd given Jewel. I growled then, my tail pointing straight up. She looked up.

"Roman?" She held the ring out to me. "Jewel told me where to find it so you'd trust me. I'm Eve."

I stared at her, at the ring in her hand. She'd known exactly where it was, so I let down my guard. I shifted back to human, and took the ring. "How is my Wild Rose? Has she received the news?"

Eve took a knee before me, and bowed her head. "She's

heartbroken. She was very close to her cousin," she said.

"Have I killed us?" I asked. "Does she have a message for me? Will I see her again, or face the darkness without her?"

"She says to wait for her," Eve informed me. "She'll be here at the time you agreed. If she's not, then you have to run."

Run? Without her?

"How could you kill another wolf?" she asked. "Even an enemy?"

I hung my head. "My heart only saw hate when the sight of Mason's body threw grief over me," I said. "A life for a life, I had to kill my beta's killer. Tyler was trying to kill me, and Mason died to protect me."

She shook her head sadly.

New footsteps approached. "Who else did you bring?" I asked.

"No one. I would not betray Jewel," she confirmed.

I sniffed at the air, recognising the new arrivals. Not wolves.

"Roman, I'm here with Spencer," Solstice called out. "Will you let us in? We're here with a message from your parents."

I handed Jewel's friend the blanket. We never had to cover ourselves from other wolves, but I thought it respectful to cover her with people she didn't know. She wrapped it around herself.

"Come in," I said.

They entered the cave. Mason's blood still stained Solstice's hands. The sight of it squeezed my chest again. Both Spencer and Solstice frowned at Eve.

"You're a Silver Moon wolf," Spencer said. "Is this your mate, Roman?"

"No, she's not," Solstice added before I could say anything. "She's not the one I saw."

"She's not here to hurt me," I said quickly. "My mate sent her with a message." I forced a smile. "What news do you bring from my alphas?" I asked.

Spencer and Solstice glanced at each other. *Uh oh, this isn't good.*

"They want you to present yourself before them, and surrender your claim to alpha." Solstice said. "I couldn't talk them out of it."

"The only way the Silver Moon Alphas will allow you to live, is if you leave," Spencer added. "So your parents told me that you must be banished. That's an alpha order and cannot be ignored."

Banished. A fist of fear gripped my throat, and I couldn't breathe.

"Where will I go?" I asked. "I've known this farm my whole life. This is my home. To be banished is worse than any punishment. Can they not chain me up, restrict me from shifting?"

Spencer and Solstice gazed down at me with pity. "Banishment or death," Spencer said. "I'm sorry, Roman."

The cave spun. *Banishment.*

"Jewel will join you," Eve said. "Where you go, she will go too."

"You have until tomorrow morning," Spencer said. "Silver Moon and Midnight alphas agreed for me to ensure you leave."

Tomorrow morning. Since I'd mated with Jewel, I'd not felt a part of my pack, but it was supposed to lead into me accepting the mantle of alpha. Not to become a new pack. A pack of two.

"Thank you for giving me time," I said.

Spencer reached a hand out to me. "I'm sorry, kid."

I shook his hand. Solstice hugged me tight. "At least he had some happiness before he died," she added. "He died keeping his oath, Roman. Protecting you."

"Did you see his death?" I blurted.

"I did," she acknowledged.

I was glad she wasn't trying to act as if she didn't know what I was talking about.

"At my parents' house, you said pain and tragedy," I recalled. "You saw all of this. You saw Jewel, too." I turned my focus to Eve. "Can I do this to Jewel? Force her into banishment with me?"

"You're not forcing her," Eve said. "This is her choice."

"Why banishment?" I asked Spencer. "Why not just give up my title without being banished?"

"You took a life," he replied. "To your people, to your deity, life is sacred. You must bear the burden of what you've done, and the punishment that goes with it."

The declaration was a crushing weight. His choice of words sent a chill through me. Vampires didn't value human lives, seeing them only as food. I wondered how many lives Spencer had taken. Did he know the meaning of the word, 'burden'? I pushed the thoughts aside. He and Solstice were as much part of my life as my pack were. I'd known them as long as I could remember; even as a cub, they'd had a lot of involvement with my parents. In a way, they were my pack, even though they were friends to both Silver Moons as well as Midnight wolves.

"Will I be cursed?" I asked Solstice.

She shook her head. "I don't know; your Goddess doesn't speak to me. That will be for her to decide."

My shoulders slumped, and heat rose to my face. I was ashamed that I'd broken everything. I'd never felt so defeated in my life

"You haven't lost that alpha spark of yours," Solstice added. "You can start a new pack. You already have betas who swore oaths to you."

I was afraid to look at her. Afraid to hope. "They wouldn't leave the pack for me." I still couldn't believe Jewel would.

Solstice gave me a smile. "You'd be surprised what your betas would do for their alpha. They've always been your pack, Roman. That's a tradition of your people that dates back centuries. The five of you…four now, have always been your own pack within the Midnight wolves. For the survival of the pack, the next in line usually takes over leading the pack. But there are times when up-and-coming alphas have to form their own pack, find their own territory. With your betas and your mate, you won't be a lone wolf."

I said nothing as the two of them left. Only Eve remained. She'd been silent during the interaction.

"There are some wolves who might follow Jewel too," she said. "She means a lot to them, and they've been part of her pack for years. They're more wild than she is, though."

Wilds. Would they follow an alpha from another pack? We had our own Wilds that chose not to shift.

"Thank you for bringing me hope with her words," I said. I opened my hand, the ring sitting in my palm. "I will wait for her. Will you join us if we form a new pack?"

She shook her head. "I will not leave my mate and cubs behind. I like you, Roman, and if I were as young and carefree as Jewel, that might have been a possibility. She is like a sister to me. Please take care of her."

Without another word, she dropped the blanket and shifted into a silver wolf, reminding me of Mason, and she ran.

I sat down. I had never considered leaving our territory for another. I had no idea where to go.

Chapter 19

ROMAN

The valley was flooded with sunlight. Birds were singing, and I stopped to drink from the river. As I left, I marked my territory at the foot of a tree. The angle of the shadows showed it was still a couple of hours until the sun would set. I lay down, soaking up the heat from the sun, and dozed off.

The engine of my ute woke me. I slinked up the hill to find Gideon, Bennett, and Tobias. I eyed Tobias and his crutch as Gideon helped him from the cab. Gideon's hands lingered on Tobias, their eyes locked.

"I'm okay, Giddy," Tobias said.

Bennett held grey trackies and my green Swanndri, indicating he needed me to shift. Hesitant to leave behind the joy and freedom of being a wolf, I lay down.

The three of them took a knee in front of me, Tobias leaning on his crutch.

"We're still your betas," Bennett said. "You're our alpha, and we're with you. We go where you go."

Finally, I shifted and accepted the clothes Bennett handed me. "I can't ask that of you," I said.

Bennett grinned. "You're stuck with us, bro! Mason would have followed you too."

A lump in my throat stopped any words. The light fading in Mason's eyes, his final words, would haunt me for a long time.

"We're here to bring you to the funeral," Gideon said, breaking the awkward silence. "The alphas have permitted that, at least."

The lump in my throat spread to my chest, cutting off air. "I have to be here at midnight," I said. "Jewel is returning then."

Bennett led me to the ute. "The funeral starts when the moon rises. You'll be back in time. We'll get everything ready in time for the morning."

I let Bennett drive, not in the mood to do much more than stare out the window. Banished, and a killer, the two words hung over me like a dark cloud.

"Any ideas on where we're going?" Tobias asked. "I still have a day or so before I can shift."

It didn't matter where I went; I'd have my betas, and my mate. I shrugged.

"I'll pack our bags," Bennett offered. "We can throw them in the back. And our bikes. We might need a trailer or something so we can take them all."

"Leave Mason's bike," I said. "Oh, and can you find a jacket and helmet for Jewel?" I slightly cheered at the idea of taking her for a ride on the back of my bike. Maybe when I saw her at midnight we could ride.

"The shops will be shut when we finish the funeral. But Mason has a couple of ladies' jackets and helmets," Tobias said. "He got them so he could take wolves for rides."

I couldn't hold back the laughter then. "That sounds like him," I said.

Bennett elbowed me. "He was so convinced he'd be the first to find his mate, he got the wolves fucking tattooed over his ribs."

I nearly choked. "That's what that was? I thought he was just being crude."

Gideon scoffed. "He was. Nothing he did wasn't crude. He was a charmer, though. Even the humans couldn't look away from him. In fact, didn't a human man try to pick a fight with him that one time, because his woman was paying more attention to Mason?"

The cab filled with our laughter.

Bennett stopped the ute, his laughter fading. "The whole pack will mourn him, but it was us that knew him best," he said. "We were his brothers. We shared a bond that no one else in the pack could have dreamed of experiencing."

"They had a reason for calling us 'the troublesome five,'"

Gideon recalled. "From the moment of our first shift, we were trouble."

"With a capital T," Tobias agreed. "If you hadn't been our alpha, Mason would have been the leader of our brotherhood. He's solely responsible for half the messes we got into."

I glanced over at Gideon. "That reminds me. Why didn't any of you stop him from marking his territory on Silver Moon land? You had to know Tyler would be pissed."

"You know as well as I do, there was no stopping Mason once he got those ideas," Bennett said. "He pissed on the very same tyre that he slashed. Also, I love the work he did on Tyler's chump mobile; those claw marks were really deep! Besides, Tyler was more pissed when he heard your howl. He knew you were hunting."

I shook my head in amusement as the ute started moving again. The sun had set; it wouldn't be long before the funeral started.

We reached the house and climbed out of the cab. Bennett and I undressed and shifted.

"I'm staying back with Tobias," Gideon said. "We'll meet you there!"

Unsure how the pack would react to my presence, I stuck to Bennet's side as we moved around to the back of the house. It was tradition for wolves' funerals to be where they lived. In normal circumstances, as his alpha, I should have led the service.

The smell of death hit me. One by one, wolves approached Mason's body, and each let out a spine-chilling howl. The sound of grief carried across the land, punching me in the chest. I hung back, and watched Tobias limp to Mason's body. He lowered his face into Mason's fur. When he lifted his head, his eyelashes and cheeks were wet. "You did what you were supposed to do." He spoke as though consoling his dead kinsman. "What we all took an oath for. We thank you that our alpha is still alive. We'll take it from here, brother."

His crushing words crashed over me. I was glad to be a wolf at that moment. When Tobias stood back, Gideon lowered himself, his face also in Mason's fur. "Run with your ancestors," he said. "May the Goddess watch over you."

My parents advanced on Mason's body, each wrapped in blankets. "Mason was beta to the next alpha in line," Dad said. "In the morning, our son will give up his title by leaving the Midnight Pack. Until then, he is still part of the pack, and has come to mourn his beta. He will howl to send Mason on his way. Then the pack will add their voices to his."

"Mason was loved by every member of our pack," Mum said. "The day he took his beta's oath, was his proudest day. His parents were just as proud. They have a few words."

Bennett glanced at me when Mason's Mum and Dad stepped forward. His dad was a beta to my Mum.

"No parent expects to lose their cub," Mason's mum said. "The pain of such loss is unbearable. His last action was exactly what he swore to do. While we maintain our place in this pack, we surrender to our wolves. We will join the Wilds."

It was not unexpected. But it still shocked me that Mason's parents would shift one last time, and run with the Wilds. So much within the pack was forever changed. I whimpered, to find Tobias's and Gideon's hands on my back, Bennett nudged at me with his head. Mason's parents shifted. They would never again take human form.

Then it was my turn. I approached Mason's body, wolves lowering their heads as I walked past them. Bennett howled. I nudged at Mason.

"Roman must be the one to attempt to rouse his beta," my dad said. Everyone knew this part.

I nudged at Mason again, my heart splitting open. I nudged him a third time, human tears escaping my eyes. Sorrow flooded in.

"Now he will howl, and call upon the Wolf Goddess to take him to the Eternal Forest," Mum added.

I lifted my nose to the sky, putting all my grief into my howl. It echoed; a mournful sound. I took in a breath and let out a second howl. Bennett's voice joined mine. Then my parents'. Then Mason's parents'. Soon, the entire pack was howling, our voices expressing sorrow.

Wolf Goddess, take him to the Eternal Forest, where he can run with his ancestors, and those who have died before him.

Our howls died down. I nudged Mason into the shallow hole that my parents would have had someone dig earlier. Wolves carried branches over, covering him.

I commit his body to the ground. He lived a life with nature; now he returns to nature.

"Now Roman will lead a hunt in Mason's honour," Dad said, and he and Mum shifted.

Chapter 20

JEWEL

Howls rose from the pack. I listened from a small distance away, Eve beside me. I let my mind wander. Roman would also be farewelling the beta Tyler had killed. I still couldn't believe Tyler had killed someone. He had a temper, but murder was not something I could have imagined. The hatred between our packs should not have escalated to such an extent, and wolves on both sides were feeling the effects. The loss.

Goodbye, cousin. I remained in disbelief that I was leaving my territory. Land I had spent my entire life on, to be with the wolf who'd killed my cousin. That I'd fallen so hard and fast for that wolf, and he had fallen just as hard. I couldn't hate Roman; he'd be feeling the consequences of killing.

I resisted the urge to howl, in fear of who would take offence by my presence. As the mate of our next alpha's killer, I would be unwelcome. Eve howled for the both of us, her voice reverberating through me.

May the Wolf Goddess guide you to the Eternal Forest. Once again, I yearned to howl, to express my grief as the rest of the pack were. Instead, the pain exploded through my entire being. I let out a whimper, and Eve nudged me under my jaw. I nuzzled her. It was time to leave. It would still be a few hours before midnight, but I could wait in the cave. Away from the pack that now hated me.

Eve ran with me, the Wilds following at a distance. As we approached the valley, I stopped, scanning our surroundings. The leader of the Wilds moved forward, pressing her head against mine. The others surrounded us. She turned to leave, followed by the rest, leaving me with Eve.

Eve whined, and pressed against me, lifting her paw to my back. A very human gesture, but my heart swelled with affection. She turned, following the Wilds back to Silver Moon territory. They stopped once, turning back before disappearing into the forest. I howled. Their own howls echoed back in return.

I sniffed the air and the ground, getting used to the new

scents. This valley was mostly untouched by wolves. There were plenty of deer, rabbits, and possums that passed through frequently. I recognised where we'd hunted. The scent of blood had soaked into the ground. A new scent, strong. Roman had marked his territory, the strong smell of a pack I now belonged to. Our new pack. I found a nearby tree, marking it as my territory. I'd never claimed territory before, and it thrilled me.

Finally, I entered the cave. The blanket lay on the ground. It didn't take me long to uncover the ring Roman had given me.

"You're early." Roman's voice echoed in the cave.

I turned around, letting my mouth fall into a smile. He was dressed in the leather jacket I'd seen him in the first time I laid eyes on him. His own grin widened, and sheer joy glinted back at me from his yellow eyes.

"I heard you howling." He placed a helmet and jacket on the ground, holding clothes out to me. "What do you say we go for a ride? My bike's parked at the top of the valley."

Excited, I shifted, and Roman helped me dress. His clothes were too big on me but I didn't mind. He then pulled the jacket on me.

"It smells like another wolf," I said.

"Mason took other she-wolves on the back of his bike," he said. "I hope that's okay. I can get you your own jacket when we get to wherever it is we're going. Humans close their shops at night, so I didn't have time to go into town to get one yet."

"I'm sorry you lost your beta." I comforted my mate, wrapping my arms around him. "Do you want to talk about him?"

He didn't move, except for his arms sliding around me, his chin on my shoulder. We stood like that for a moment that stretched out. "He died protecting me," he said finally. "Tyler meant that knife for me."

I pulled back, wiping the tears from his face. "We will honour Mason," I acknowledged. "If we have cubs, our son will be named for him."

He tilted my chin up with the crook of his finger, pressing his forehead against mine. "I'm sorry I killed your cousin," he said. "I don't know what came over me. I saw Mason dead, and just wanted to kill him. I've never felt rage like that before. I can't say I ever want to feel that again." He let out a deep breath. "Now I fear the Goddess will curse me.... I deserve to be cursed. I killed another wolf in anger. Humans kill each other; we don't."

The Curse! I'd always thought it was just something made up to scare cubs. Would that really happen to him? I gazed into his eyes. There was an emptiness there. A helplessness. The smile I'd seen when we first met was nowhere in sight.

"Come on," I said. "Lead me to your bike."

We walked side by side, Roman's fingers closing around my hand. I was getting a sense of how affectionate he was, but his grip expressed a need to comfort me too.

"This is a beautiful valley," I remarked, hoping to lift both our moods.

A river, a forest, with a perfect view of the mountains. I wished we could have made our home in this valley.

"There's plenty of hunting, a river," he agreed. "The hot spring. We wouldn't have been in need of anything else."

I laughed. "Cave-dwelling wolves."

He shrugged "Anywhere with you is my home. Cave, or in the mountains, I don't care." We stopped, his eyes roaming over my face. I yearned to provide solace to him, so I stretched up to kiss him. His lips were soft, his mouth warm as I slipped my tongue in. He responded instantly, caging me in with his arms. His tongue teased at mine, and our hearts thundered in rhythm with one another. I ran my fingers through his hair. His embrace tightened, almost as if he were desperate to hold on to me. I was just as desperate, afraid if I let go he'd disappear.

Breathless, we gazed at each other. He ran his fingers through my hair.

"If I'm to be cursed, you're the light of the full moon in the darkest night," he whispered.

I cradled his cheek, his beard rough against my hand. "I'll guide you through your darkness. Don't let it bury you. Stay with me in the light."

The smile he gave was a shadow of the one he'd given when we first met.

His thumb traced from my chin to my lip. "Are you ready to ride your first bike? I can go slow if you want."

As we started to walk again, he paused, sniffing at the air. His nose led him to the tree I'd marked. "You've marked your territory!" he said. "Jewel, you were born to be an alpha." He pushed stray strands of hair from my face. "Are you okay being my co-alpha? My betas will accept you." His eyebrows drew together. "There's no one else for me, but I don't want you to feel forced into this."

I leaned against him. "You couldn't force me into something I didn't want to do if you tried," I asserted. "I've beaten you in a fight already; I'd win in that one too."

He beamed down at me. "Oh, is that so?"

"I marked you before you could mark me," I reminded him. "You were hunting me, and you couldn't find me."

"You should run!" he declared, a hungry glint in his eyes. "I'll show you!"

I laughed as I darted up the hill, with Roman only a few steps behind me. His deep rumble of a laugh was close enough for his breath to tickle my ear. His arm wrapped around my waist and we hit the ground. As he lowered his head, the roughness of his facial hair brushed against my cheek. He nibbled at my ear, my neck. I squirmed under him. My whole body reacted to his presence, and I wished I was naked. I moaned, tilting my hips enough to grind against him.

Roman groaned, his lips brushing my throat, up to my lips. His breathing and scent had changed, indicating his lust. "I would love nothing more than to stay here," he growled. "To take you under the stars." He kissed me again, pushing his hips down, both of us grinding against each other. "To tear off your clothes. I would love to give chase to you. to claim what is mine, to feel your soft skin against mine."

"Then do it," I breathed. "You've already marked me. I'm yours, Roman; why do you hesitate?"

"I want to take you for a ride first. To feel you against my back, your heart vibrating against me. To feel the speed of the bike. For you to experience your first ride on a motorbike."

I lifted my head, closing my teeth over his jaw.

"Then, when we return, I have a chase planned," he added. "You knew the forest the first time. I know this valley as much as I know my own territory."

He stroked my hair as he gazed down at me.

"I'm starting to think you just like chasing things," I commented.

Roman slowly climbed to his feet. "Maybe I do."

He helped me up.

His hand rested on my hip as we walked up to the bike. "What if I want to do the chasing?" I asked.

"We can do whatever you want. I have to admit I do like the sound of you chasing me," he revealed.

I leaned my head against his shoulder. "Your presence is so calming. I'm a little scared about leaving, but you have a serenity that makes me feel like it's okay."

He smiled down at me. "That's who I've been taught to be," he said. "The Midnight alpha has to be the calm one, with reason. To walk the peaceful line, inspire the pack."

We approached the bike. "Tyler was a real hothead. My aunt and uncle always had trouble with his temper." I turned my eyes up to Roman. "He was protective of me, and always gentle, a side very few saw."

Roman's eyes darkened. "I'm sorry," he said again, in a genuine tone.

I nodded, pulling away from him. I didn't want to think about my cousin. Nor the wolf my cousin had killed. "I just want our packs to not hate each other," I blurted. "None of this should have happened. We wouldn't have to meet in secret. No one had to die."

A tear slid down my cheek.

Roman squeezed my hand. "I know."

I forced a smile. "Let's ride! I need a distraction."

He handed me leather gloves, and he helped me with my helmet before putting his own on.

"I like this look on you," he said, his voice muffled in the helmet. He lifted his visor. "You do look hot in leather."

I didn't like the feel of the helmet, it was somewhat restricting, but I pulled up my visor. "I definitely think I have a thing for the biker type," I admitted. "No one on our territory had bikes, but I saw plenty of movies at Eve's."

I melted at his grin, my insides quivering.

"Ok, there's a few things I need to show you, when riding on the back," he said, and shut his visor again before pushing mine down, too. He held the bike steady. "Grab the bike, and climb up and across," he said.

I did as he said, feeling awkward. When I was in place, he climbed on with ease.

"Hold on," he encouraged. "Mold yourself into me, and put your hands on my waist."

I relaxed into him and rested my head against his back, wishing the helmet wasn't in the way of his warmth.

The bike started, and I jumped in fright. He chuckled. "Sorry, she's a noisy beast, but she's a good ride."

I tightened my grip on his waist, and the bike started to move slowly.

"I just need to run through something with you. When I turn the bike, I lean," he explained, and leaned a little to the left. "When you feel me lean, you need to move in tune with me, and lean when I do. It makes for a smooth turn, and we won't wobble and lose control."

"Okay," I agreed.

We did circles for a few minutes as he guided me. I kept my eyes on where we were going. I had to admit I did enjoy the feel of the bike's vibrations, and the firmness of Roman's back.

"Good, you're a natural at this!" he said. "Are you ready?"

"I think so?" I said.

He patted my hand on his waist. "You'll be okay, Jewel. I won't let anything happen to you. Just don't lean against the turn."

It wasn't long before we reached the road, and we were flying. The scenery blurred by. Joy bubbled up.

"Are you okay?" he asked.

"I am," I replied. "This makes me want to howl."

"I'll never hold you back from doing that!" he said with laughter in his voice.

Then, he let out a howl. My wolf rose to the surface and responded with her own howl. Bursting with happiness, I laughed. I would be safe, and loved, with Roman and his betas.

After a while, he slowed down, and I stared at the houses on either side of the road.

A strange scent overwhelmed me. "What's that smell?" I asked.

He slowed to a stop, breathing in. "Cows," he said. "Silage. Cow shit." He pointed. "These are dairy farms. That one has chickens." He pointed again. "That one has pigs."

I shook my head. "No, it's something else. I can't explain it. It smells a little unnatural. My wolf doesn't like it."

"Ohhh," he turned in his seat. "You've never been near a human dwelling, have you?"

"No," I confirmed.

"What you're smelling is humans," he said. "I don't really like being among them all that much either. We can't be ourselves around them."

He climbed off the bike, and helped me off. We removed our helmets, and he wrapped me in a warm, strong embrace, his chest against my back.

"Plus, they frown upon not wearing clothes in public," he joked. "They have some stick up their ass about it. I suppose it's just not natural to them."

Soft music drifted from one of the houses. "Oh, I know this song!" I said.

Roman twirled me around, his eyes in shadow as he smiled down at me. "Have you ever danced before?"

Chapter 21

ROMAN

Our bodies pressed together as we swayed in time with the music. Jewel had one hand on my hip, the other on my chest, and her head rested on my shoulder. Our shared grief earlier that night still clung to me. I wanted to see her smile. So without warning, I spun her around, caught her in my arms, and dipped her. Laughter burst from her, joy shining from her eyes as she grasped my arms tightly.

"Are you afraid I'll drop you?" I asked.

She shook her head. "No. I just like holding your arms. Your muscles."

"The life of a farmer," I said.

She slid one hand down my arm and under my tee-shirt. I gasped, reaching for her wrist. "Oh, cold hands!" I laughed. "How about we wait until we're back in the valley before you do something like that?"

"Why?" she asked. "Does it distract you?" A glint of mischief shone from her eyes.

I pulled her hand from my abs. "No. It makes me want to strip you down and do a different kind of dance with you. One that the humans wouldn't appreciate if they caught us."

We danced more. Or I should say we swayed more. I knew nothing about dancing, but had seen the humans in romantic movies move like this. Jewel started to shiver and I pulled her hard against me, hoping to warm her. But if I was to be honest, I was just as cold as she was.

"Come on," I whispered. "Let's get back and warm up."

We returned to the valley. As I pulled her helmet from her, I laughed at the pink in her cheeks and the glee reflecting from her eyes. "I told you you'd enjoy that," I said.

"I did!" she agreed with excitement. "I hope we do that again! I loved being pressed against you!"

"I have to admit that certainly added to the enjoyment of the ride for me," I agreed. I'd found a riding partner as well as my hunting partner. I took my helmet off, placing it on the seat of my bike, and started to undo her jacket. "Now about what I promised you earlier."

Her hand reached up, closing over my fingers. We gazed at each other, not moving or blinking. Then very slowly, she guided my hand down, the zip opening her jacket. She shrugged the jacket off, folding it over the bike. Her fingers grasped the zip of my jacket, which she pulled down. Her hands slid under my jacket, pushing it off.

"Taking it slow, are we?" I asked, desperate to tear her clothes from her, and give chase.

She glanced up, her eyes filled with light. "I want to take my time," she said. "I want to enjoy the need I have for you. To stretch it out before we're naked against each other."

I growled, my wolf rising to the surface. I wanted to chase, and mark her again. But a new nature was rising. More dominant, rough. The alpha. "And I want to push you up against that tree," I told her. "I want you howling." I reached for her, sliding my hands under my tee-shirt I'd lent her. "I want this tee-shirt off you, now." I firmly grasped her chin with my other hand. "Now."

She smirked at me. "I'm sure the alpha in you would love to be obeyed. But I will be as much an alpha as you. So, you'll just have to be patient." She grabbed my hand. "Are you alright with that, or do I have to stretch this out more?"

Oh fuck. I both loved and hated hearing her talk like that. My alpha spark was blazing, which meant she would probably be feeling it too. I brushed my hand over her stomach, placing it on the small of her back. I pulled our bodies together. "Still want to take your time?" I asked.

Instead of replying, she continued her bizarre slow strip-tease. She took her time to lift my tee-shirt over my head. Her hands ran over the tattoos on my chest, stopping on the moon. "I want a tattoo," she said. "Both of our wolves. Running, side by side."

"I'll talk to Solstice," I said. I could barely stand it. I removed her tee-shirt.

"Slow," she said, and her hands reached for my belt.

"You're tormenting me," I panted.

Despite the cold, her body this close and my own need, warmed me.

"Instead of seeing it as torment, enjoy it," she said. "What do you feel?"

"Deep yearning," I admitted. "And the cold."

"Hunger," she threw back at me.

I nodded. "I want to chase you so I can mark you again."

She pulled my jeans down. I kicked them off. My briefs went next. She stepped back.

"My mate, in all his naked glory," she said, her eyes on my cock.

I gave her a look up and down. Her skin was smooth, pale. I cupped her breasts, and caressed her body. "My mate," I said, "in all her beauty. Let me help you out of those jeans."

I eased them off her, and she took a step away from me. "Now chase me," she said, and shifted before darting down the hill.

Fur rippled across my skin. This time it didn't fade, as I wasn't holding my wolf back. I didn't wait for the shift to finish before I was on all fours, dashing after Jewel. My canines lengthened, and claws grew from where my fingers had been. My mind became one with the wolf, instinct and hunger overpowering. She'd teased me, building up my hunger for her, my need to have her. In wolf form, it was more than just lust or desire. Those were human feelings. No, what I felt went deeper. A carnal craving compelled me forward.

She darted out of my way when I almost reached her. Determined, I turned just as quickly, growling softly. She put speed into her run, and gained more of a lead. I relaxed into the hunt. I'd let her believe she had the advantage. It would stretch the hunt out, adding to the anticipation for both of us.

She gained more of a lead.

'Are you even trying?'

The voice in my head made me stumble. *What the fuck was that?*

'Wait, you heard me?'

It was her voice. I was hearing her voice. *'I hear you,'* I replied.

The mate bond. That must be it. That meant the Wolf Goddess really had been the one to bring us together. She'd bound our fates to one another. This was an incredible revelation. Joy burst in my chest as it dawned on me that we really were fated. There was no one else for me, but her.

'Oh, don't let that distract you,' Jewel said. *'You're supposed to be chasing me. It's not fun if you don't put effort into it.'*

I dug into my alpha strength and speed. She had not yet received that gift, so it would make me faster than her. With a burst of speed, I caught up. I pushed her to the ground. *'It's called a chase. I wanted to stretch it out,'* I said. *'But if you insist, I will claim you here, on the ground.'*

She twisted out from underneath me and was on the run again.

'The big, bad alpha isn't very good at this. Maybe I should chase you?' Her laughter inside my head was strange. It would take awhile to get used to this.

'You'd like that, wouldn't you?' I shot back as I bolted after her.

'Actually, yes!' she declared. "Why should you have all the fun?"

I chased her through the forest, loving the skill with which she managed to avoid capture. I had to admit she was good at dodging and evading me. Her weaving was unpredictable. The thrill of this game only added excitement.

Finally, I caught up to her again. This time when I pinned her below me, I put all my weight on her. *'Now try to escape,'* I said, my teeth bared.

'No, I think I'm happy. Looks like I was wrong, you did put effort into it.' Even in my head, the lust seeped through. *'Here, or the cave?'*

She rolled over, gazing up at me, her eyes fierce. I more than hungered for her. My needs were of the wolf, ferocious. I backed off, letting her stand before closing in again. We had mated in human form. Now we were to fully complete the ritual, truly connecting us as one. Her body under mine didn't resist as I claimed her. Locked together, I was complete. She was mine, and nothing could take her from me now. My wolf impulses had taken over, the ache I'd had soothed, my rough movements quickened. A savageness pulsed through me, and a deep satisfaction.

'Mine.' My voice took on a low growl. A possessiveness I'd never experienced before filled me.

I was her alpha.

'Mine.' Her voice was just as possessive.

She was *my* alpha. I howled as we reached completion. Jewel's voice added to mine.

I released her and darted forward, nipping at the back of her where I'd marked her.

ROMAN

Jewel snuggled into me. Having a warm body pressed against mine filled me with bliss. Lulled into a relaxing state, I closed my eyes. We'd taken shelter in the cave, and I was safe, warm.

I woke to the sounds of human voices. Bennett's and

Gideon's. I kept my eyes closed.

'*Your betas are here,*' Jewel whispered in my mind.

'*Ignore them,*' I said back. '*Maybe they'll go away. I'm too comfortable.*'

"Awww, look at the two of them," Bennett said from the entrance to the cave.

"She doesn't feel or smell like a wolf from another pack anymore," Gideon added. "They've completed the mating bond. She's a part of his pack. Our pack."

"Mason would have loved to have seen this," Bennett added.

I couldn't help myself. The pain, still fresh, overwhelmed me, and I whimpered. Jewel nuzzled at me. I opened my eyes.

"Sorry, man," Bennett said. "I shouldn't have said that. I just miss him. He's been a part of our lives for so long, it's hard to get used to."

I lifted my head to meet his eyes. Grief weighed down on me, and I wasn't sure if I was drowning in it, or being crushed by it.

"I know." Bennett walked over and sat on the ground next to me.

Jewel whimpered and moved away.

'*Are you okay?*' I asked her.

'*I don't know them, I'm not used to people I don't know coming towards me so fast,*' she explained.

I growled at Bennett as a warning. He backed off.

"We just need to borrow our alpha for awhile," Bennett said, eyes on Jewel. "We'll bring him back in about an hour."

I got up. '*Wait here,*' I told her. '*I won't be long.*'

'*I'll be here,*' she replied.

I followed Bennett and Gideon from the cave, stopping at the entrance to turn around. Her eyes were on me. I hesitated.

I didn't want to be away from her.

'*You are the other half of my soul,*' I said. '*I'll see you soon.*'

'*You are the one I didn't know I waited for,*' she said.

I hesitated again. '*Do you want me to leave one of my betas with you?*'

'*Roman, just go. I'll be okay. If I get bored, I'll go running or use the hot spring.*'

Reassured, I turned, and hurriedly caught up with Bennett and Gideon.

"You two look like you're made for each other," Gideon said. "The two of you lying together like that just looked so natural. You wouldn't think you'd only known each other for a couple of days."

Has it been two days? I really felt like I'd *always* known her. I'd heard stories about how quickly the mate bond connected those fated to be together. That it was only natural for me to fall for her so quickly.

We reached the top of the hill where my ute was parked next to my bike. Clothes were scattered around. I took human form and started to dress when I noticed Tobias in the back of the ute. I gave him the chin raise in acknowledgement. My clothes were damp, so I hoped I'd have a chance to get changed.

"Did Jewel enjoy the ride you took her on?" Bennett asked. "Looks like you were in a hurry to strip off when you got back."

"Actually, it took far too long for my liking," I confided. "She wanted to stretch it out." I glanced at Bennett. "What did you need me for?"

Bennett reached into the cab and threw my Swanndri at me. "Your parents want to see you."

My breath caught in my throat. "They want me to abdicate? I thought we had until morning for that."

"You do. They want to say goodbye."

Emotions rose up that I wasn't ready to face. My banishment had become real.

"They do?" I asked in disbelief.

"You're their only son, Roman. Of course they want to see you before you're banished," Bennett confirmed.

His words hit home. As alphas, my parents' first duty was to the pack. But they were still my parents. I couldn't deny I'd miss them as much as the rest of the pack. My chest hurt. I really was leaving my home, my pack. To have Jewel going through the same only added to the crushing guilt.

I climbed in the ute, this time behind the wheel. Most of the drive was quiet.

"What's going to happen for the next alpha?" I asked as we reached the alpha house.

"Your banishment means there will be a challenge for leadership," Bennett said. "The next wolf in line would technically be me, but I'm your beta. And you haven't died, so there would be no passing of the spark."

I walked inside, my betas behind me. This would have been my home, with Jewel. To the right of the entrance was a wing reserved for betas and their mates. Underneath was the den in which we'd all grown up together.

"Roman." My mother's voice was relaxed. "You smell different. Like you're no longer part of our pack."

Mum wore a long black jacket over her clothes. The alpha in me recognised her as another alpha, watchful.

I nodded. "I suppose I'm not," I agreed. "I'm advancing to alpha, and I've just been banished instead of succession."

Hurt flared in her eyes.

"I'm sorry, son." Dad entered the room. "We had no choice.

Had you been killed by Tyler, we would have demanded the same thing. The Silver Moon alphas are grieving. We were lucky to talk them down from demanding your death."

"I get it," I reassured them. "I know, it wouldn't have been an easy decision. But it leaves the pack vulnerable. What will you do if someone challenges you?"

Mum hugged me. "Don't you worry about that. Just be careful."

Dad nodded. "Especially as you're taking someone who is very likely to receive the alpha spark after Tyler's death."

That hadn't occurred to me. "Do you think she will?" Bennett was just as likely to, in my death, so I couldn't deny there was a possibility. "She's a Wild, though. While still part of the pack, they're not really considered alpha material," I said.

"She's the niece of the current alpha. Next in line *by age.*" Dad said.

We reached the living room. Mum's betas were there, waiting with their mates. Bennett's, Gideon's and Tobias's parents. The place where Mason's parents once stood; empty. Another reminder of what we'd all lost.

I considered this. "What if she received the alpha spark? She's still my mate. I don't think the Silver Moons would want that," I pointed out.

Mum sat down on the couch, and Dad took his place next to her. "I've contacted my sister," she said, changing the subject. "There's an unclaimed territory near where she lives that would be perfect. Lots of forest, undeveloped. Her pack has offered to help you build houses. No humans go that deep in the forest, so you'd be safe."

"Does she know I've been banished?" I asked. "About everything?"

Mum nodded. "I had to tell her why."

"Her pack is still willing to help? Knowing I've taken a wolf's life?" To kill another wolf was unforgivable.

"They have. Her alpha says it will be for the best. You know the stories about what happens to a wolf when they've killed. About the form you could take under the light of the full moon. Or if angered, hurt, or even aroused."

"The curse," Gideon muttered.

Tobias met my eyes. "If the curse is real, would his bonded mate be cursed, too?" he asked Mum. "Mates experience the other's pain. Would this be passed to..." he stopped in mid-sentence when Gideon elbowed him.

"It's the second night of the full moon," Bennett said. "If it was to happen, wouldn't it have happened already? They're just stories."

"Stories are often shared through the generations as a warning," Dad explained. "There's usually truth to them. We don't know if that's the case with this, as no wolf has killed another for *centuries*." He rubbed his forehead. "In response to your mate, there is a possibility. It may alter her shifts, like yours."

I stood up. "I have to go."

"I'm sure she's fine," Mum said. "Roman–"

I ran from the house, ignoring my parents' voices as they called after me.

My betas ran after me. "Bennett and Tobias, finish packing. Gideon, come with me," I commanded.

I barely waited for Gideon to get in the ute before I started moving.

Chapter 23

JEWEL

I listened to Roman and his betas leave, the cave empty, silent. I already missed his warmth, his presence. A warm, caring energy that encased me, leaving a cold emptiness in his absence. I'd sensed his remorse through our new mate bond, and forgiveness had flowed through me. I hoped he had felt that. With no idea how long before he returned, I explored the cave. There was the main cave at the entrance, and the larger cavern with the hot spring. I found a tunnel, and followed it to another large space. There was no other scent in there, only Roman and his betas. They'd each marked their territory here, so I did the same.

I was no longer part of the Silver Moons. The separation saddened me. But I still wouldn't change it. As part of a new pack, my future held mystery. I wandered around the cave again before going outside. I sniffed at the ground. Without thinking, I let out a howl, filled with joy. Surprised by the returning howls, I turned towards the sounds. *The Wilds!* Unsure why they were this close, I howled back. While Roman was away, we could run.

Their howls got closer. I ran towards them, elated. They saw me and rushed forward, circling and sniffing at me. I leapt up, and spun in circles, showing I was in a playful mood. The leader of the Wilds let her mouth widen into a smile and dashed past me. The valley filled with our yips, whines, and howls as we ran.

We were between territories, but had the entire valley to run. A male wolf approached me, sniffing. When he got too close, I growled and he backed off. The leader of the Wilds licked at my ear, panting from the run.

A familiar scent that I didn't expect wafted over us. I turned, watching the wolf as he kept his distance, hanging back. I was unsure why he was running with the Wilds. I'd seen him with them once before and didn't know his reason. Was his obsession with me getting a little out of hand? He'd risked it coming here; he must have known Roman was away.

It dawned on me slowly. He knew Roman had left. Which

meant he'd been *watching.* How had I not picked up on his scent earlier? The wolf noticed me looking, and approached. He sniffed at me, but I moved away. The leader of the Wilds started to watch him, moving between the two of us. Had she picked up on my anxiety about him being here?

Playful with the other wolves, I let myself relax. We drank from the river and ran back towards the cave. I howled again. This time, Roman howled back. Overjoyed, I turned towards where I knew he'd come down the hill. His return brought relief, as I was hungry, and wanted to hunt with him. I hoped he'd let the Wilds hunt with us. This time, they didn't react as they had before at his approach. Maybe they sensed who he was to me.

Parker barrelled towards me, and before I could evade him, he knocked me to the ground. I tried to get out from under him, but his teeth closed around my shoulder. I froze. A deep, menacing snarl filled the air before a black shadow moved fast, throwing Parker off me. I rose, shaking myself off. Roman and Parker fought, growls and snarls echoing in the forest. The Wilds backed off.

I shivered. Something was wrong. Before I could get very far, I stumbled.

One of Roman's betas approached me in human form. "I'm Gideon," he said. "What happened? Are you okay?"

I shifted, so I could speak. "Parker bit me," I said. "I think he marked me."

Gideon examined my shoulder. "Yep, that's deep. A mark." He frowned. "Roman! He marked her."

Roman's growls were a low rumble that echoed across the valley as he faced Parker. Pain radiated in my chest, and I shivered at the sudden cold. A wolf could only be marked *once.*

No wolf had received the mark of two. Gideon helped me to my feet, his brows furrowed. He pulled his green jacket off and wrapped it around me. My legs buckled, but Gideon caught me.

"Shit, this is not good," he muttered. "I'm taking you into the cave. You need warmth."

"Roman," I muttered. "My alpha."

The only answer was snarls and growls as Roman and Parker fought. Darkness crept up and I fell into nothing.

Chapter 24

ROMAN

The link between Jewel and myself had weakened a little. She passed out in Gideon's arms, his jacket around her. Wolves I didn't recognise approached Gideon tentatively, their focus on Jewel. It was possible they were the Wilds of the Silver Moons.

"I'm getting her into the cave," he called out. "The blanket in there will keep her warm."

She needed more than warmth. She needed Solstice. There was a reason a wolf could not be claimed twice. To mark a wolf who'd already been marked, especially by their fated mate, had the potential to *kill*.

I turned my attention back to the wolf. He lunged at me and I dodged him, turning around and closing my jaw on his flank. He yelped and snapped his jaws, snarling. I bared my teeth, crouched my belly low to the ground. As he leapt at me, I flipped my body over, latching on to the underside of his leg. His pained whimpers didn't stop him from trying to break free.

We circled each other, canines bared. I seethed, rage twisting in my gut. The overwhelming need to kill was a jolt deep within my heart. The same fury that had overcome me when I gave chase to Tyler. This dark desire was unnatural, but it was as if once I'd killed, I'd never be rid of that. I only wanted to protect my mate. He lunged, and my jaws snapped, just missing his throat as he darted out of the way of my teeth. His jaw closed on my hind leg, eliciting a yelp from me. I pushed him off with all my strength, and he hit a tree. He didn't move. I stood over him, his eyes on me as he whimpered.

"Roman!" Gideon shouted from the cave entrance. "She doesn't look so good. She needs help. She needs you!"

I took human form, and when the wolf who'd marked Jewel lunged at me, I punched him with all of my strength. He went down hard. *Good.* Ignoring the biting wind and freezing air, I rushed towards Gideon, taking Jewel from him.

"Call Bennett!" I told him. There wasn't enough time to send him back to the house. "Tell him we need Solstice. Now!"

He pulled his phone from his pocket and called, putting the

phone on speaker.

I led Gideon towards the cave, worried about the tremors passing through Jewel.

"Hey," Bennett answered after one ring.

"Bro, you need to get Solstice down here, now!" Gideon almost shouted. "Jewel has been bitten. Marked by another wolf."

Inside the cave, I placed Jewel on the blanket, wrapping it around her.

"On it!" Bennett said and hung up.

"Hold on, my beautiful Wild Rose," I whispered. "Help is coming."

I was naked and cold. My clothes would be in tatters halfway down the hill. I'd felt the moment that the wolf had bitten her. Not just the pain, but the way our link had fractured. I'd known something was wrong and bolted down the hill, ready to kill.

Her breathing was rapid, and she groaned in pain. I squeezed her hand, panic swelling in my chest.

"She's mine." A voice came from behind us, at the entrance to the cave. "I marked her."

I spun around. The wolf had shifted. The sight of him awoke a new hatred. "You cannot mark a wolf who has already been marked," I growled. "The only thing you've done is hurt her. Maybe worse."

I didn't know who this wolf was, and I didn't like the helplessness that threatened to close in. Black fur rippled across my entire body, and my rage mixed with my protectiveness of Jewel. I wanted to kill him. I didn't care that I wasn't supposed to. I didn't care that as an alpha I should be calm. Electricity jolted through me, and I let out a roar. Pain lanced my fingers when claws shredded the flesh. The tingling of the shift felt stronger this time. Harder to hold back. So I gave in to it. A darkness rose up, but instead of falling onto all fours, I towered over Gideon. His eyes widened.

"The stories are true," he whispered. "Roman...you're the beast...I don't..."

I didn't stop to hear the rest of what he was saying before I turned to charge at the other wolf who'd marked Jewel. He glared at me, and the scent of his fear only added to the crackling storm swirling inside me.

I wasn't human, but I wasn't a wolf, either. My arms and hands had grown in size, my height almost doubled. Curved claws and bulging muscles followed by a rippling power that I had never experienced. Intoxicated by it, I roared. I advanced on my opponent and slashed at him.

"Roman, stop! you need to calm down." Gideon shouted, and ran at me.

I pushed him away, focusing on the other wolf again.

"I'll tear your throat out," I said, my voice deep, thunderous. I lowered myself onto all fours and ran at him.

When I hit him with the full force of my body, the unmistakable crack of something breaking only urged me on. I pinned him down, claws at his throat as I pressed down on his chest. He struggled to breathe, another crack, his chest giving way under my strength. I smiled, baring my mouthful of fangs.

"She'll hate you if you kill me," he gasped. "You already killed her cousin. Mate or not, she'll never forgive you. Look at what being a killer has turned you into. You've brought a curse down onto yourself, and her."

I removed the pressure on his chest and let out a roar that vibrated through every bone in my body.

He growled, but didn't move. I swiped at him and he hit the wall. I followed, but he managed to dart out of my way. I was twice his size, but he was faster. I ran at him, canines bared. He stood his ground, and I collided with him. Tyler had run; this one wouldn't. It was as if he were fighting for the same reason I was. He'd just marked her, and he thought he had a claim to her.

We circled and lunged at each other. I yelped as he swung at me, striking hard. Tired of the fight, I lunged, leaping at him. I landed on his chest.

"Roman, stop!" Bennett had arrived. "Don't kill him."

It was too late. I struck fast, tearing into his throat. Flesh came away, and blood gushed from the gaping wound.

"Roman!" Gideon shouted. "Stop!" His voice was heavy with desperation

I turned to find Gideon bleeding. Had I done that? I ran to Jewel. Her heartbeat was faint, her breath shallow. I took human shape. "My love?" I whispered, grasping her hand. "I can't lose you. Not now." I caressed her face, kissing her. My chest ached. Tears streamed down my cheeks. Loss stole my breath. "Wolf Goddess, don't take her from me yet," the words fell from my lips and I couldn't hold them back. I would do anything to hold Jewel in my arms. To have her running at my side. "I will sacrifice my human side just to run with her for the rest of my days. She is my hunting partner, and I will not let you take her from me."

"Don't anger the Wolf Goddess," Gideon warned. "After you killed again, I don't think she's going to favour you right now."

I turned my attention to Bennett. "Where is Solstice? I told you to bring her," I demanded.

"She's on her way!" Bennett assured me. "I told her where

you'd be, and I came here as fast as I could."

I kissed Jewel again. Her skin was pale. There was no response from her. Her heartbeat was faint, slow. Solstice would be too late.

"She's dead," I whispered, and buried my face in her neck.

Chapter 25

ROMAN

Wolves howled from outside the cave. Background noise, as I pulled hair from Jewel's face. I couldn't breathe, and even my wolf was torn apart. The crushing weight of grief was almost too much to bear. Tears streamed down my cheeks.

"Why would the Wolf Goddess bring us together, only to do this?" I demanded, my voice breaking. "We were supposed to have years together."

Bennett's hand touched my shoulder. I flinched. Adrenaline that had swamped me now faded to nothing.

"The Goddess and the stars blessed our union, only to leave me empty," I said. "I defy them both!"

"Don't say that!" Gideon said, his shoulders tight, body rigid. "Roman, you killed. *Again.* She's going to be angry with you."

I had killed *again. Twice* a killer. No wonder the Goddess sought to take my soul from me. "My heart was complete. Now fate has torn it from my chest," I whispered, stroking Jewel's face again.

I found the ring I'd given her, a reminder that even by human ritual we were united. I slipped it onto her finger

I lay down beside her, embracing her.

"Roman, I'm sorry," Bennett said.

"Where is Solstice?" I asked.

"She could not bring Mason back, it will be the same with Jewel," Gideon said.

"I don't want to hear that!" I growled.

Pain tore from my chest and I howled, putting all my anguish into it. I'd lost Mason, but now Jewel lay before me, her body still. The sorrow that whirled inside me was like a wild ocean, Churning and threatening to drown me.

The Wilds outside howled in response. Gideon and Bennett let their own howls loose.

"Roman, she's not dead," Solstice's voice took me by surprise. "Listen carefully. Her heart still has a very slow beat. It's because *yours* still beats." She walked into the cave. "She is dying, though."

The Wilds entered the cave behind Solstice. Then Spencer. "You can help her!" I declared.

A Magic Wielder and a vampire had the power to save my Jewel.

Solstice approached, and knelt at Jewel's side. I sat up. She held her hand over Jewel's chest, murmuring words in another language, closing her eyes. When she opened them again, she met my gaze.

"This is not something my Goddess can do," she said finally, her words piercing my already shattered heart.

I glanced up at Spencer. "Then you help her, Spencer. Please!"

He shook his head. "I will not turn someone without their consent, kid. You know this."

Helplessness held me prisoner as I stared at my dying mate.

Solstice lay her hand on my chest. "We can't help her, but *you* can."

Hope blossomed in my chest. "But I'm not alpha yet," I said. "There's been no succession, nor a ceremony recognising me as such."

Solstice shook her head. "You don't need that to be alpha. You were born with the alpha spark. You are powerful. Your strength makes you unique compared to other wolves. Roman, you have the ability to bring her back with your alpha bite. But you should know–"

Hope sparked in my chest; a blazing inferno. I didn't hesitate, didn't care about the warnings she tried to give me, her words fading into the background. I tapped into my alpha spark and leaned forward, my canines large in my mouth. I shifted into the wolf, and I licked Jewel's forehead. Gideon's jacket was in the way, so I pushed at it with my muzzle. Behind me, the

Silver Moon Wilds whined and lowered their heads. I closed my jaw over her shoulder, the very same place that now dead wolf had marked her.

I barely noticed paw steps on the cave floor echoing behind me. More wolves entered. My parents' scent filled my senses. I tuned them out. I needed this to work. More howling sounded outside the cave. Energy pulsed deep within, a response to my pack's presence. Jolted by the surge from within, I willed it to flow into Jewel. It didn't occur to me that I shouldn't feel them. Warmth spread over me, the essence of my wolf listening to me. Darkness crept up, and voices echoed inside the cave.

I let her go and stepped back. Jewel didn't move. I nudged at her, letting out a whine.

'*Get up,*' I pleaded, unsure she could hear me.

I flopped down beside her, no longer able to hold on to that hope as the last of it left me. The Goddess had taken from me. Heartbroken, I rested my head on her and closed my eyes.

"Roman?" Bennett's voice was close, and he ran a hand through my fur. "Roman, it's okay."

I didn't open my eyes. I no longer had the energy for anything, my strength extinguished to nothing but an ember. Given freely to save Jewel's life.

"Roman, open your eyes," Solstice said.

Her tone was urgent, but drained and grieving, I longed to sleep.

"Will it help?" Mum asked.

Her question made no sense, and Solstice's response was lost in my own consciousness slipping away.

"I concede to the new alpha of the Midnight Pack," my mum's voice rang out. "In the eyes of the Wolf Goddess and my pack, I recognise the succession. I kneel to my son, Roman."

I opened one eye to see the entire pack around me, kneeling. The Wilds bowed their heads. No longer able to hold on, I slipped into unconsciousness.

A hand ran through my fur. Then a second. The body under me moved, sitting up. I was lifted into Jewel's lap. She leaned forward, kissing the top of my head. My heart skipped. She was alive! It had worked!

"Roman," Jewel's voice shook, weakened. "Roman, please open your eyes."

I only had the energy to let out a grunt.

She stroked me again, lifting my head up. "Roman, please get up." She pressed her head against mine. "Roman, please."

Her anguished voice pierced me. I opened my eyes to find hers close to my face. She kissed my muzzle. Her eyes were silver.

'I would die happy taking that kiss with me,' I whispered.

Jewel laughed. "It's not time to die yet, and there are plenty more kisses to be had. You're now the alpha of your pack. It seems I am, too. Passed on from Tyler's death. The alphas have recognised that."

"Roman, the line of succession has been passed down. Look upon your pack," Bennett said.

I lifted my head, taking in my surroundings. Every wolf in the cave had supported my becoming an alpha, and slowly my strength returned. The alphas of the Silver Moons were at the cave entrance, also on their knees, their eyes yellow. Had they accepted Jewel as alpha? My parents' eyes had also changed from silver to yellow. The alpha spark blazed within. Midnight Wolves and Silver Moons had new alphas.

Chapter 26

JEWEL

One month later

Spring was on its way, and my body surged with the energy of the soon-to-rise full moon. A month had passed since we almost died. Still haunted by taking two lives, Roman struggled to accept his own actions. His fear of the beast he'd become plagued him with nightmares. There were times when I could almost feel it through our bond. And the closer we got to the full moon, the stronger it became.

I walked into the den into which Roman and his betas had moved our bed. The den he had grown up in, claiming the house when he ascended to alpha. He sat shirtless on the side of the bed, staring at the wall, his eyes showing his torment.

"Roman?" I approached him slowly, speaking with a soft voice.

He looked up, and the lost glimmer in his silver eyes turned to joy, beaming at me. "Jewel, my Wild Rose. You light up the darkness."

I stood in front of him, wrapping my arms around his shoulders. His slid around my waist, as if he were holding on for dear life. The two of us didn't move for a few minutes. He took deep breaths, burying his face in my stomach. I squeezed him in my embrace, and kissed the top of his head. Roman growled against me, then fell back onto the bed, taking me with him. I laughed, attempting to squirm from his grip. His arms tightened. I gazed into his face, finding his big, goofy grin as his eyes gleamed with tenderness and love.

The way he looked at me still filled me with warmth. As if at that moment, I was the only one in his world. He lifted a hand, pushing hair from my face, tucking it behind my ear. I lowered myself, kissing him His lips were soft and warm, and his hand slid up to the back of my neck. The next kiss was hungry, full of desire, his tongue teasing mine. Deep need for him churned inside me.

Engulfed by an inferno, I ground against his erection. He lowered his head to the bed with a groan. I nipped at his throat, his shoulders, kissing the mark I'd left a month ago. His fingers found their way to the back of my neck. My hands ran over his body, as my lips found his again.

His hand moved under my tee-shirt, caressing my body. I pressed against his chest, wanting to nuzzle him.

"Your clothes are in the way," he murmured against my mouth.

I stripped off without hesitance, and Roman chuckled.

"The moon will be up soon," I said. "Gideon said he's going hunting with Tobias and Bennett."

He smiled up at me. "Do you want to join them?"

I returned his smile. "No, I'm happy here with you."

He ran his fingers up and down my back. "Mmmm, I don't want to move from here, either," he admitted.

I wanted more, so I reached down, wrapping my fingers around his cock. Precum leaked from the tip. I stroked him.

"Three guesses what you're after," he said, amusement and yearning shining through his eyes. His fingers dipped down, pressing against my clit, rotating, and I pressed myself against them. He slid two fingers in, curling them. I whimpered when he pulled his hand away, licking my arousal from his fingers.

"Already so wet." A long rumble vibrated through his chest. "Lie back. I want to look at you," he panted.

I lay back, gazing up at him as he pinned me beneath him. Then he moved down, dropping kisses to my body. I held the back of his head as he moved up, his lips leaving a blazing trail. He sucked each of my nipples, then reached my throat, nipping lightly.

"Roman," I gasped. "I need you–"

I didn't finish my sentence before he pushed inside me. My body pulsed around his erection, waves of heat spreading throughout my body. I wrapped my legs around him, holding him tight as he almost pulled out, before driving in again.

"My Wild Rose," he panted.

I bit at his jaw. "My romantic alpha," I said in return.

I moaned as a shiver of pleasure raced up my spine. Another thrust sent a second shiver, his cock hitting deep. I closed my eyes.

"Open your eyes," he commanded. "I want to look into your eyes as you come," Roman whispered in my ear, then nibbled at my earlobe. "I want to see the pleasure that I give you."

I lifted my gaze, aching to touch him. My hands moved over his ribs, digging my nails into his back. Warmth wrapped around my heart, radiating out. Our grunts and my moans mixed with the slapping of our bodies.

The locked eye contact, his warm body moving against mine, his hardness inside me, all pushed me racing towards an orgasm. I opened my mouth, whimpering his name. Roman grabbed my jaw, dropping his head to kiss me roughly. Waves of elation pulsed through my body. He pulled me into his gaze again, his silver eyes wide open.

"Fuck," Roman grunted. "I'm close, Jewel."

"So am I," I gasped. Tremors travelled from my spine to my pelvic muscles, and my toes curled.

Roman kept my jaw in his grasp as we came. Before we could recover from that release, fur covered his arms. Through our bond, I sensed the beast in him rise to the surface. While the Wolf Goddess had blessed our union, she had cursed him for the lives he had taken. He'd been fearing this the last month. He was about to shift.

"Fuck," he groaned, and pulled out of me.

I stopped him climbing off me, wrapping my arms around him, using strength in my embrace.

Fear glinted through his eyes. "Jewel…"

"Shh, it's okay Roman," I reassured him.

Through our mate bond, I drew on the power of the beast, pulling it into myself. Embracing that was like grabbing an electric fence and holding on to it as power surged through my body, while also looking into darkness and having something look back.

His mouth opened.

"What are you doing?" he demanded.

"We share the curse," I growled back. "I will not let you face this alone."

He gazed into my eyes, his love shining through. "Are you sure?"

I called upon my beast within, and struggled to hold her back.

I reached up to cradle his face. "I'm sure."

"Goddess, I love you," he said, his eyes lighting up with his smile. "You really are the light of the moon in the darkest night. And the stars."

"And you light up any room," I returned, and let the shift wash over me.

My black fur spread across my skin, my teeth shifting in my mouth, filling it with rows of long, sharp teeth and canines. My muscles and body expanded. More powerful than a normal shift, my body numbed through the transition. I glanced down, seeing my new shape, energy surging through my muscles.

He stopped trying to hold his beast back, his own shift mirroring mine. The growl that came from Roman was more feral, savage. His face had contorted into that of a wolf's, his entire body covered with his black fur. His canines were longer than normal.

'I want to run!' I told him. *'I want to howl at the moon!'*

On all fours, I bounded from our den, the fresh air caressing my skin. Roman leapt after me, tackling me to the ground. I snapped at him playfully, aware of the new strength in my jaw. I'd have to be careful.

'*I want to chase you,*' Roman said. '*Get ready to run!*'

I pushed him off me. '*I believe it's my turn to chase you,*' I declared. '*Get ready to be hunted!*'

He nuzzled me, his giant head pushing me over. I laughed.

"Woah!" Tobias's voice drew my attention.

He and Gideon stood over us. I smiled up at them.

"That's fucking awesome!" Gideon said. "So are you two lovers going to come hunting with us, or do you have your own thing going on?"

Bennett came from the house. "Sorry to interrupt. I have a report from the boundary," he said.

Roman stood to his full height, which in his current form had to be at least seven feet tall. I stood next to him, not much shorter.

"That's going to take a while to get used to," Gideon said.

Bennett met my eyes. "Your Wilds wandered over the line again. Our Wilds have joined them. Cubs are loving it." He grinned. "There's a silver wolf with them, two cubs with her."

Eve! She must have taken her cubs from their den to bring them here. Since I'd joined Roman's pack, she'd snuck over a few times. The Wilds had settled in the valley between pack grounds, wandering over the line whenever they felt like it. We took it to mean they considered themselves part of both packs.

I laughed, the sound more like a deep growl.

"Your aunt and uncle are at the boundary, asking for entrance." Bennett continued. "So are your parents."

Roman nuzzled at me. "This is your command," he said.

"They're your pack."

I'd never been raised to be alpha. But Tyler's death had changed that, the alpha spark passing to me the same time I became co-alpha to Roman and his pack. Peace had been forced from tragedy.

'You're my pack,' I whispered to him in my mind. "You're my co-alpha," I reminded him. "They're *our* pack." I turned my focus back to Bennett. "Let them in," I agreed. "But they'll have to wait. Tell them I'm otherwise engaged."

Bennett nodded, smirking at us before returning to the house, talking on his phone.

"Gideon, Tobias, I put you in charge of escorting them in," Roman said.

The pair instantly shifted, their wolves darting away towards the boundary.

"Where were we?" Roman asked me, his teeth bared.

"You were running," I reminded him.

Without a word, he lifted his head towards the moon, and let out a deep, guttural howl. Unable to hold back, I let out my own. Wolves around us howled back. Then on all fours, Roman ran.

Epilogue

ROMAN

Twenty five years later

Jewel stood beside me as we watched five cars pull up. The pairing ceremony would be the following night, and packs were already starting to arrive. Silver Moon wolves approached at the same time.

"Where's Mason?" Jewel asked. "He should be here to welcome them as the next alpha in line."

"I'm here," Mason said from behind us.

"Where's your sister?" I asked.

Mason shrugged. "Probably running with the Wilds. She wants nothing to do with this."

"Evie gets that from her mother," I commented, grinning down at Jewel. "Are you ready, Mason?"

Mason stared at me for a moment, his eyebrows drawn together.

'*He looks just like you when he does that,*' Jewel said through our bond.

"You'll be fine," Jewel encouraged our son. "Go and welcome them. You've got this, Mason."

"Where are your betas?" I asked.

Mason's betas walked from the house. "We're here! Ready!"

"You should be ready without Roman having to question your whereabouts," Bennett told his son. "At all times!"

Gideon chuckled. "Don't be a grouch."

Gideon's daughter with Addison, and Tobias's son with Sienna laughed. The two of them had always been close, and it was very possible they were mates. Gideon and Tobias loved the idea.

Mason and his betas stepped forward to welcome the alphas, who were now getting out of the cars. International packs. The national wolves would be arriving in the afternoon.

"He'll make a good alpha," Tobias said. "He has so much of you in him."

"He's already irresistible to the she-wolves," Gideon added with a wink. "Channelling some of his namesake."

"I never really met him, apart from that one time," Jewel said.

"But Roman was the irresistible one to me."

Tobias sighed. "He would have loved to see the next generation," he said.

Silence engulfed us as memories of my beta washed over me.

"Even if he'd mated, he would have always shared his bed with many," Bennett added.

"Oh, for sure!" Tobias said. "Gideon and I may be mates, but we're happy with Addison and Sienna, too. The four of us share a bed often."

"Dad, I would like to introduce you to Felipe," Mason said, approaching with the alphas in tow. "Felipe is from Spain. And this is Lucas, from England ,and Angus, from Scotland." He pointed to female alphas. "Kayleigh is from Northern Ireland, and Dalia from Egypt."

"Thank you for travelling so far," I said. "Please, come inside. I have organised a hunt tonight, and we have some more local packs arriving this afternoon." I said. "Celebrations will begin when they get here."

Spencer's scent announced his arrival, and I turned, frowning.

"You have a vampire here," Dalia said. "You know they're at war with the humans."

The world had changed a lot over the last five years. The vampire king had declared war with vampire hunters, bringing them from the shadows. In the process, wolves, other shifters, sirens, and more of the paranormal world had been discovered.

"I know," I acknowledged. "Spencer is not part of that war; he poses us no danger. He is protective of both packs here."

Spencer stopped before me.

"Spencer, have you come to join in with our ceremony?" I asked. "I can't say we've prepared for your presence. You don't hunt animals, so I think you'll have to bring your own food."

"I must speak with you," he said, taking in the crowd around him. "Damn, it's been a long time since I've seen this many packs in the same area." He turned to face me again. "Can we speak? Alone?"

'*This looks serious,*' Jewel said through our mate bond.

"Mason, perhaps you can take our guests on a tour of the grounds," I said. "I apologise, my friends. I will leave you all in the capable paws of my son. I will join you shortly."

Mason and his betas led the new arrivals away.

"Spencer, what is it?" I asked.

Spencer met my eyes. "We should go inside."

I led Spencer inside, Jewel at my side. My betas followed.

Spencer sat in the chair opposite us. He leaned forward. "You're aware of the war," he said.

It wasn't really a question, more an indication of the subject he'd come to discuss. But I nodded anyway.

"I'm aware," I agreed. "I worry about the day the local humans realise we're here. A community that has always welcomed us may not be so friendly."

"Vampire warriors have landed in America." Spencer pointed out. "Luis plans for an assault on Washington, D.C, that he will oversee himself. He will install his own generals in place of their human government."

I leaned forward. "Why are you telling me this?"

He looked around at each of us.

"What does the term, 'The Immortal Wolf' mean to you?" he asked.

"A vampire who helped my pack centuries ago," I replied. "I'm aware he sent you to watch over our pack when we started to migrate."

Spencer smiled. "Our people have lived in peace because of what The Immortal Wolf did for your ancestors. Natalia was a powerful alpha, and she declared him to have a place in your pack. She said if he *ever* required anything of her pack, they would help in *any* way needed."

I looked at him. "Did you know her?" I asked. I knew the stories of Natalia. Of her ferociousness and strength, leading her pack when wolves were hunted by humans. Carlos had killed humans who went after Natalia's pack.

"Why are you bringing this up now?" Jewel asked. "If he is coming here, we will welcome him. He is part of our pack; we will not turn him away."

"Why would he come here?" Tobias asked. "Wouldn't he be fighting in the war?"

Spencer met my eyes. "Natalia promised him if he *ever* had need of her help, of her pack's help, he only needed to ask," he repeated.

Goosebumps raised on my arms. "Say what you're going to say," I commanded.

"The Immortal Wolf asks for your help," Spencer declared.

Roman and Jewel will return in Bloodking.

Acknowledgements

To my mum, who continues to support me in my writing career. You have always encouraged my writing, and I'll never forget that. I'm glad you don't want to read my romance books!

As always, Jess, you have helped me so much along this journey. I appreciate all that you do. Bouncing ideas off you, plus you have helped get me through imposter syndrome and times I just didn't feel worthy. I will always appreciate our late-night chats.

To all my alpha and beta readers: Michelle, Jess, Nicole, and Daphnee: your feedback will always be valued, and I appreciate having you all on my team.

Alicia, aka the "best assistant evah!" You weren't just there online as an ARC reader, but an in-person friend and unofficial assistant. I look forward to the many adventures at upcoming events.

Ellen, my editor who has edited (and re-edited) every book I have written now. We met in person at Emerald City Comic-Con ten years ago now, and built a friendship over fandoms and GISH. I would never have imagined at the time that you'd be my editor. Funny how the world works, isn't it?

To my readers who not only buy my books, but also follow my journey and come to my signings. You have really added to my writer's journey, and your support helps push me to be a better writer.

About the Author

Serra is an author of dark historical fantasy and paranormal romance books with stories that draw you in from page one. Within these worlds that she created, you will find unbreakable family bonds, darker aspects to humanity, shadow realms as well as passion, lust, strong FMCs and men who would risk anything for the women they love.

Serra's journey to becoming an author started from a young age, when her first creative writing attempt—a poem titled 'The Mighty Oak Tree,"—was published in her primary school newsletter. An avid reader with a vivid imagination, her Mum always encouraged her to keep writing. She proceeded to write poetry and short stories before discovering a deeper passion for novel writing and screenplays.

In 2021, she adapted a screenplay she'd been working on, into her debut novel 'The Shadow Within,' which was published in November 2023.

Serra is a Melbourne-based author from New Zealand. As a reader and a writer, she's drawn into the dark fantasy and paranormal romance genres. Like many authors, she balances her writing alongside a day job in which she works in the communications part of a marketing and digital team; by night, she's a weaver of words, creator of worlds bringing forth stories that hold readers captive.

If you wish to subscribe, please visit:

www.serrarosewrites.com

Be the first to receive updates and sneak peeks at character art, quotes, chapters, next projects and early access to pre-orders.

Also by Serra Rose

The Horsemen Chronicles:
The Shadow Within
Death's Shadow

Upcoming Titles in The Horsemen Chronicles:
The Whispers of War
The Echoes of War
The Scourge of Famine
The Plague of Humanity

The Bloodsong Series:
Bloodsong
Consumed

Upcoming Titles in The Bloodsong Series:
Bloodking

The Bloodsong Series Spin-offs:
Lovestruck
Eternity
Lovesong